MW00513316

WATER BATH CANNING COOKBOOK FOR BEGINNERS

Complete A to Z Knowledge about Preservation, Pressure Canning, and Safety Procedures to Make Delicious and Mouthwatering Jams, Pickles, and Meals in a Jar Recipes

KAYLA BLANTON

© Copyright 2022 - Kayla Blanton
All rights reserved.

The content contained within this book may not be reproduced, duplicated or transmitted without direct written permission from the author or the publisher.

Under no circumstances will any blame or legal responsibility be held against the publisher, or author, for any damages, reparation, or monetary loss due to the information contained within this book, either directly or indirectly.

This book is copyright protected. It is only for personal use. You cannot amend, distribute, sell, use, quote or paraphrase any part, or the content within this book, without the consent of the author or publisher.

By reading this document, the reader agrees that under no circumstances is the author responsible for any losses, direct or indirect, that are incurred as a result of the use of the information contained within this document, including, but not limited to, errors, omissions, or inaccuracies.

Please note the information contained within this document is for educational and entertainment purposes only. All effort has been executed to present accurate, up to date, reliable, complete information. No warranties of any kind are declared or implied. Readers acknowledge that the author is not engaged in the rendering of legal, financial, medical or professional advice. The content within this book has been derived from various sources. Please consult a licensed professional before attempting any techniques outlined in this book.

TABLE OF CONTENTS

INTRODUCTION 1

CHAPTER ONE 4

  What Is Water Bath Canning? 4

    Pressure Canning 5

    Water Bath Canning 5

    Why Is Water Canning Necessary? 5

    When Is The Right Time To Use A Water Bath Canner? 7

    Home Canning Benefits 8

CHAPTER TWO 13

  Water Canning Supplies 13

    1. Must Haves 13

    2. Optional Items 19

  TIPS FOR PURCHASING THE SUPPLIES 21

CHAPTER THREE 23

  WATER BATH CANNING STEP-BY-STEP GUIDE. 24

    PREPARATION 24

  HEATING 26

  COOLING 27

  STORING 27

  CHOOSING THE COOKING SURFACE 28

  WATER BATH CANNING RULES 31

CHAPTER FOUR **34**

WATER-BATH CANNING RECIPES 35

    Jams Marmalades, Chutneys, and Jellies 35

DESSERTS 42

PICKLES... 45

TOMATOES 49

CONDIMENTS... 54

    Meals in a Jar 58

CHAPTER FIVE **72**

WATER BATH CAN LIMITATIONS 73

    Food Type Limitations.. 73

    Altitude Problem 73

    Temperature Issue 74

    Combination Recipes Limitations..................................... 74

    Strict Details.. 74

    Time-consuming 75

    Broken jars and seals... 75

    Less Nutritional Value 76

Items That Cannot Be Water Bath Canned................... 77

    Foods That Cannot Be Canned 79

Water Bath Canning Mistakes To Avoid 81

    The Equipment.. 81

    The Pre-Processing 83

    Processing 84

The Post-Processing 85

CHAPTER SIX **87**

WATER   BATH   CANNING   SAFETY
CONSIDERATIONS 88

Kitchen Safety 90

Food Safety 91

Food Preservation Safety 91

Temperature Management 92

Cooking Temperatures 93

Pounds To Kilograms 93

Pesticides 94

EWG's 2021 "Dirty Dozen" 95

EWG's 2021 "Clean Fifteen" 96

Vegetable And Fruit Water Bath Canning Charts 98

CHAPTER SEVEN **101**

TYPES OF CANNERS 102

Water Bath Canner 102

Pressure canner 103

Choosing Canners For Water Bath Canning 103

Canning Storage Tips 105

CONCLUSION **107**

FAQs 108

THANK YOU **111**

INTRODUCTION

Food canning is not an ancient preservation technique. The origin of food canning can be traced to the late 18th century. During this period, people began to heat-treat food in airtight containers or jars as a good alternative to preserving food by drying, salting, and fermenting them. It came up more as a necessity, just like other problem-solving inventions of the past.

When Napoleon Bonaparte challenged thinkers in 1795 to create a reliable method to preserve food for his gallivanting army, a French confectioner, Nicholas Appert, took on the challenge. Using some of the existing local ideas of homemakers, he would later succeed in preserving food items by sealing them in glass jars placed in boiling water. It has since been one of the safest and most reliable ways of preserving certain foods, particularly those with high acidity. We can call this short history the genesis story of food canning as we know it today.

This book is about this technique of food preservation but from a narrower angle: water bath canning. The process of canning is simply packaging food in jars to preserve them. This means a jar of food can sit on a shelf without refrigeration and still be good months or even a year later.

There are two recommended canning methods, including water bath canning and pressure canning. While pressure canning is used for low acidic food, water bath canning is recommended for food with high acidic foods.

Without a doubt, the displeasing stories of canning could make you decide against it without giving it a trial. You hear of jars exploding, jars not sealing properly, and that serious illness called Botulism. The reality is that there shouldn't be anything to worry about as long as you are armed with the proper information.

This book provides in-depth information about everything you need to know about water bath canning. My ultimate goal is to take you by the hand through this preservation technique.

That is why in Chapter Three, I have designed an easy-to-follow, step-by-step guide for newbies to water bath canning. The good thing about guides of this nature is that they offer well-researched, precise information about the subject. It eliminates guesswork and provides empirical details. This book is a product of years of experience in home canning and research from reliable sources. One thing that makes it stand out from the rest is that, as the author, I have been where you are at some point, a novice who is anxious about the whole thing.

Just before the step-by-step guide to water bath canning, I provided a background to the technique in Chapters One and Two to provide a background to the method. The essence of this is to get you acquainted with substantial information about the topic and provide the context needed to help you see why processing your food for long-term storage is important. I can imagine that you know some stuff already. But then, the possibility of you missing out on some details is still there.

Chapter Four is all about water bath canning recipes, with some of them categorized into breakfast, lunch, and dinner. Does water bath canning have limitations or downsides? You'd find out about that and more in Chapter Five. Chapter Six is about safety considerations around this food canning technique while Chapter Seven is about choosing the right canners for water bath canning and other related extra information.

Lastly, I have conducted extensive research and compiled the questions many people are asking about water bath canning. So, I end the book with an FAQ section. In this book, I have emphasized the need for you to own a book on home canning for reference. This book will help you achieve this objective.

CHAPTER ONE

What Is Water Bath Canning?

Home canning, otherwise known as canning or putting up, refers to the process of preserving foods in glass jars for as long as a year. The process involves heating the jars to kill germs or related organisms and create seals that prevent food spoilage. More often than not, the choice of jar used depends on the country. For instance, Fowler's Vacola is used in Australia while Weck Jars, Kilner jars, and Mason Jars are specific to people in Germany, the UK, and North America respectively.

As mentioned in the introduction, there are two techniques for canning: water bath canning and pressure canning. The main difference between these techniques is the type of food being preserved and, of course, the process.

Pressure Canning

This preservation technique is the only canning method recommended for poultry, meats, and other low-acid foods. It involves the use of a pressure canner which looks like a pressure cooker with a small amount of water heated at 240 degrees Fahrenheit under pressure or 212 degrees Fahrenheit with no pressure. Once the heat is turned off, the canner is opened, and the jars are removed to cool on an insulated surface.

Water Bath Canning

On the other hand, water bath canning is much easier than pressure canning. You can only preserve vegetables, fruits, pickles, tomatoes, and other high-acid foods through water bath canning. This technique involves placing foods in jars that are placed in boiling water (brought to a boil at 212 degrees Fahrenheit), usually for a minimum of ten minutes. The pot used is big enough to hold the jars submerged in boiling water.

While both water bath canning and pressure canning techniques are useful for specific reasons, our focus here is the former, which is a great way to store healthy foods safely for at least a year.

Why Is Water Canning Necessary?

Food canning is one of the results of the resurgence of interest in home gardening in many parts of the world. But in centuries past, gardeners were simply content with eating seasonally. It was a way of life but one that came with a challenge. Most fresh vegetables and fruits are not available all year round. This makes canning necessary for those that need their locally-grown foods fresh for several weeks and months after the gardening season has ended.

No doubt, gardens often yield too much food at a time. It is simply impossible to consume all before they spoil unless, of course, you want to gift them. Alternatively, you can set out the excess after harvest and store them through water bath canning for rainy days.

Broadly speaking, the necessity of water bath canning hinges on the need to preserve fresh high-acid foods beyond the season of abundance. Preserving food is a great way to stash a wide range of foods throughout the year. Whether we like to admit it or not, certain foods are seasonal and, as such, are expensive at some point. Why not buy enough seasonal foods, put them through the water bath canning process, and keep them safely in your pantry?

It is an effective method that drives out air first from the jar, and then, from the food. This is a proven way to avoid the contents spoiling. The science behind this is simple. Oxygen degrades food's nutrition, appearance, and taste after a while. Even though we hardly take note of this; there is a great amount of air in the jar already. The food you are canning contains oxygen, too. Canning through the water bath method allows you to deal with this issue. Once the boiling process is done right and you get your vacuum seal after cooling the jar, you are assured of preserving the shelf life of the food.

Water bath canning is a good way to rid food products of pathogenic bacteria like listeria monocytogenes and salmonella enteric. These are villains that could be in a food product after purchase or harvest. So, what's the science behind it? It is mostly about the food's freshness and temperature. Once put through the canning and water heating process, most of the bacteria, molds, and yeasts are destroyed.

What's more? This technique, especially the heat processing part, helps added acid, like vinegar, to permeate low-acid ingredients like cucumber and pickles. This ensures that the ingredients are safe for consumption after months of preservation.

If done right, water bath canning is an effective, safe procedure. Generally, home canning, whether through pressure or water bath methods, comes with many unique benefits. There is more on that soon. First, let's look at when we can use a water bath canner.

When Is The Right Time To Use A Water Bath Canner?

Canning is the method used to process food in a jar that you intend to keep on a shelf. It is one of the acceptable ways of preserving food domestically, next to keeping your food in a freezer or fridge. What makes canning more special than the other means of storing food domestically is the fact that you can store and keep your food fresh and ready to use anytime within 12–24 months. You can achieve this objective through the water bath method or pressure canning.

When to use either of the two methods is determined by the acid level in the food that is intended for canning. Poor color, texture, and overall quality are the likely results you will get for canning low-acid foods using the water bath canning method. It is only safe to use for high-acid foods such as fruits and vegetables (by pickling first).

As such, when you have just harvested fresh tomatoes, fruits, or veggies, or bought them from a local farm produce store, you might decide to process and store them for use many months after.

Home Canning Benefits

Now, onto some of the benefits of home canning. I have highlighted and elaborated on some of them. Perhaps you have doubted yourself about being able to get the procedures right without compromising your safety and that of your family. Truthfully, home canning is a lot of hard work marked by attention to detail, the ability to follow instructions, and patience. I am sure that after reading the following benefits, you'd be motivated to at least have a trial of your first canning experience.

- **Saves money**

You never can tell when inflation on food will increase. It can disrupt your short-term financial plans. When food becomes expensive, those you have canned for the future can bring about a huge relief. As such, picking or purchasing food in season and canning them for the near future is a frugal way to save money. Amazingly, the quality of what you are canning will remain intact for at least a year.

Yes, there's another lens through which the financial benefit of home canning can be viewed. It encourages people to get more involved in gardening. Of course, your gardens will not provide you with sufficient supplies of fruits and veggies. Some of whatever you can gather or harvest in season, however, can be preserved through other seasons. You might be saving enough money through this means.

- **Gives control**

It is hard to control what you eat when your go-to place for food purchases is the popular supermarket in your neighborhood. If you have got a healthy diet plan, stocking your food in jars will help you stay on course. With home canning, you have control over what you put in your jars and stock up for future use in your pantry.

From another perspective, home canning helps to control what to eat to live longer. If you limit your canning to the water bath technique, it would improve your consumption of fresh veggies and fruits. And, you need not travel too far to grab some of these food items. Your pantry full of canned foods has got you covered.

- **Protection against harmful chemicals**

Buying canned foods, like tomatoes, is a known long-term health risk. Most canned foods contain Bisphenol-A (BPA), an industrial chemical added to commercial products such as hygiene products, baby bottles, and food containers. The major concern many people have for BPA is that it can leech out of a drink or food container into what we consume. This provides a massive incentive for people to consider canning their own food.

You also get rid of the dangers of preservatives and additives like calcium chloride and citric acid that come with processed and canned foods. These substances, which are often adjudged safe, are used to preserve the texture and color of some foods. Calcium chloride, for example, may result in burns in the stomach, mouth, and throat, leading to extreme thirst, vomiting, low blood pressure, and stomach pain. Home canning helps to reduce the amount of intake of these substances.

- **Contributes to environmental protection**

There is never a better time to contribute our respective quotas to the protection of our environment than now. We are at the cusp of drastic climate change that could cause damage to our planet. That is why the "three Rs" mantra, "reduce, reuse, recycle", continues to linger today. Surprisingly, many people hardly ever take this mantra seriously. And, some of those who do are lost for how exactly they can contribute to saving Mother Earth. Home canning is one good way to adopt.

It gets you active on at least two of the three "Rs" easily. You get to preserve your food and REDUCE the wastage typical of pre-packed food items. You get to REUSE the jars rather than continually dispose of the cans, bottles, and other containers from the stores. No doubt, if we can cut waste domestically through the home canning of foods, we will not only save money but also indirectly protect the planet.

- **It's a fun hobby**

If you have been looking for a new hobby, canning is a good option to consider. Just look how passionate one can be about knitting, sewing, and weaving. You can get similar joy from, and passion for, putting foods in jars too. At first, you might use the other benefits listed above as an impetus for cultivating this habit. However, after a while, it becomes a hobby. Who knows, you might enjoy the experience so much to run your own YouTube channel and share it with others.

I recommend this to those who are usually busy. Those late-night "what's for dinner" and the alacrity at popping open your canned foods are a testament to the value of your newly-found hobby.

Furthermore, you can always resort to giving these jars as gifts to close friends and family during festive seasons like Christmas. Imagine all of this coming from your hobby. You become nothing but fulfilled. Who knows, you just might be inspiring the person you are gifting, to help preserve foods that can act as rare gifts.

- **It's fun and educational**

Canning is fun. That's why I recommend it as a hobby you could adopt. To make it even more interesting you can encourage a friend or family member to adopt canning, too. It has proven to be an amazing way to socialize.

But beyond that, it is a great way to engage kids on food preservation and safety. They will be exposed to elementary knowledge of how canning prevents food spoilage. It could also get them interested in developing a thing for cooking and eating healthy. This is because food preservation through this means cannot be dissociated from food safety.

- **Gives a sense of accomplishment**

Lastly, home canning is a purpose-driven activity. Just imagine you get to storing up your harvest or supplies in season and coming back to it many months later. This can give a great sense of accomplishment.

CHAPTER TWO

We have discussed the meaning of water bath canning extensively. Now, to warm our way up to the main crux of this book, which is the step-by-step guide through the processes involved, let's have a look at the supplies you need to get it done. After all, you cannot do any meaningful stuff in your garden without your tools. Right here, water bath canning is your gardening. You're going to need a few supplies, some of which are essential, while others can be used of your volition. So, I have divided the supplies into must-haves and optional items.

Water Canning Supplies

1. Must Haves

Canning Jars: This is a no-brainer, right? You have some food to preserve through water bath canning. The first thing to think of is where to store it. What comes to mind? Plastic containers, metal containers, or jar containers. Each of these groups is used to store food but when it comes to home preservation of food that is safe for everyone, only one comes recommended.

Essentially, the main containers preferred for this preservation technique are glass jars. Plastic containers are loved for being lightweight and easy to use. The metal ones are not quite susceptible to temperature changes and are just as lightweight as plastics. However, glass jars are known to have long shelf-life benefits, make canned food (if well done) taste fresh, and are devoid of corroding their content even after a long time.

There are different kinds of jars but the main ones for canning are the wide-mouth jars and regular-mouth jars. Your choice will depend on the kind of food you wish to can. Wide-mouth jars are great for whole foods such as fruits and vegetables, while regular-mouth jars work best with pourable foods like jellies, sauces, jams, and pie fillings.

Size is another aspect of canning jars to consider. The regular-mouth jar has the following sizes: 32 oz (for sauces, sliced fruits, and pickles), 16 oz (for syrups, sauces, and salsas), 8 oz (for fruit syrup, chutneys, and pizza sauce), 12 oz and 4 oz (for jams, preserves, condiments, marmalades, jellies, and conserves). On the other hand, the wide-mouth jars have the following sizes: 64 oz (for grape juice, and apple juice), 32 oz (for whole fruit, tomatoes, and pickles),

24 oz (for pickles, asparagus, soups, and stews), 16 oz (for sauces, fruit butters, and relishes).

Similarly, some jars are considered standard when it comes to home canning. For instance, Kerr and Bell seem to have taken the shine from other brands. Whichever works for you is great! Overall, I advise anyone new to home canning to stick to the recommendation in recipes.

A canner with a rack or a pot: Here's another clear no-brainer. You need a canner for water bath canning. A water bath canner is a piece of kitchen equipment that is used to sterilize preserves or canned foods. This process assures the ability of the canned foods to survive for a long time out of a refrigerator.

Water bath canners usually comprise a stainless-steel pot, a jar rack, and a glass lid which allows for easy viewing of the boiling process. But, you may decide to use an ordinary pot rather than a complete canner. This alternative is pretty much allowed. However, there are a couple of things that must accompany the pot for the canning boiling process.

First, you need to have a cover for the pot. Then, you need a rack. A rack is crucial because it makes the jars stay off the bottom of the pot. This also allows the boiling water to circulate to all the jars in the pot.

By and large, someone can safely argue that you do not need any specialized equipment other than the canning jar. Pressure canning, nonetheless, requires the use of a pressure canner, which is different from a pressure cooker. While the latter is used to quickly cook large cuts of meats, a pressure canner is used specifically for processing low acid foods for storage in jars.

Lids: I ought to merge this one with the jars rather than a standalone item on this list. The truth is that they have significance to the preservation process and are just as important as that of the jars. A canning lid is a thin metal cover with a rubber seal laid atop the jar to effectively seal it after canning.

Lids are necessary for creating and maintaining the vacuum foams after the jars had been heated. There is a sealing compound on the underside of the lid. This prevents air from entering the jar again after cooling down. Once this has been achieved, there shouldn't be any microorganisms that could re-contaminate the content and spoil it.

The two types of lids for home canning jars are the one-piece and two-piece canning lids. In some parts of the world, like many European countries and the UK, one-piece lids are common. However, only the two-piece type is recommended in the US.

The National Center for Home Food Preservation and USDA recommend two-piece metal lids alone for home canning while describing the other type as unsafe. The two-part lid has this status in the US because of its reliability and ease of use. Also, when using the lid, it makes it easy to know that the jar is properly sealed.

Here are a few rules to follow to prepare the lid effectively:

✔ First, endeavor to wash and rinse it before use.

- ✔ Ensure to leave the proper headspace.

- ✔ Clean the rim of the jar, that is, the sealing surface, before applying the lid. This is to ensure that the food does not get trapped on the rim which can result in seal failure.

- ✔ Place the metal band over the lid and screw it tightly.

Ladle (stainless-steel, preferably): A ladle is an indispensable and multi-functional kitchen tool. Even though designs of ladles vary, a normal ladle has a long handle that connects with a deep bowl at its base. The main purpose of this tool is to take out liquid from a pot and place it into another container. A ladle is also a must-have for water bath canning.

You need a ladle to fill the jars with liquid food. It will ensure that your kitchen is not too messy. The good news is that you do not need any special kind of ladle. Any normal ladle is just great for every food canning process. The essence is to ensure that everywhere is less messy while filling the jars.

This explains why my preference is a ladle that has got a pour spout—a part of the ladle that guarantees even more efficiency. Some people may consider this item unessential for water bath canning. For me, I believe home canning can be messy. I would like to reduce the mess as much as possible. A ladle will always contribute its quota to achieving this small objective.

Tongs or jar lifter: A jar lifter is required for water bath canning as well. You should expect this one to make my list of essentials. After all, we are dealing with jars at hot temperatures. Surely, you will have to pick the jar out of the canner safely after sterilizing them in a hot water bath.

Why not use an oven mitt to get that done? Since we are dealing with hot water, using a mitt remains unsafe. You need a tool that provides safety and efficiency instead. A jar lifter is specifically designed for this purpose.

The tool is a metallic set of tongs that include a heat-resistant coating to protect the fingers. It was designed with the capacity to grip either the body of the jar or the cover. Despite the wetness of the jars, the lifter always gets a firm grip on the sides. There is a 99.9% assurance that once the jar lifter gets a good grip, each jar in the canner will be removed safely.

A jar lifter is sometimes referred to as a canning tong. Now, someone may tell you to get a tong for your canning if you are new to this business. It is instructive that you note the kind of tong to procure. For water bath canning or pressure canning, a jar lifter is a tong you need. Other types won't work.

Funnel (plastic or stainless): You might be wondering what a funnel is doing in this must-have compilation. Well, it serves the same goal for me as a ladle. As much as I love water bath canning with a substantial part of my heart, I shiver at the potential mess it can bring out. To limit the workload of cleaning the whole place after canning, you should get a funnel. So, for me, it is a must.

Another benefit of using a funnel for canning is that it prevents wastage. You tend to work faster and without the worry of the liquid inadvertently seeping away. Also, you want the rims of the jars as clean as possible while using the water bath technique.

You can choose a funnel made from any of the common non-reactive materials like stainless steel, silicone, or plastic. I have a preference for stainless-steel funnels because they are easy to clean afterward. Generally, a canning funnel comes recommended because they were specially designed for that purpose.

Kitchen towels: Ordinarily, a kitchen towel is one of the essential kitchen paraphernalia. It is used for many reasons including cleaning and drying hands, cleaning spills, drying utensils, dusting or drying vegetables/fruits/herbs, and handling hot utensils like pots just to name a few. You won't get many people to agree that it is a must-have for water bath canning pots. Specifically, you can use a clean kitchen towel to set hot jars on the countertop for cooling. It is also necessary for wiping the rims of jars before proceeding to seal them.

So far, you must have noticed that I am a stickler for cleanliness during culinary activities. This item is on this list for that sole reason. Beyond that, you never can tell when your kitchen towels might come in handy.

2. Optional Items

Home canning book: You are going to need a reference point to do justice to your water bath canning. It doesn't matter whether you are a newbie or someone experienced in this particular food preservation technique.

Without a doubt, people who are enamored with cooking at home find books and other related resources indispensable. They are good quick references on recipes and processing times. Look for a canning book with canning techniques and detailed recipes for the foods you intend to can.

Food strainer: A food strainer is a metal or wire-mesh kitchen sieve that is used to separate liquids from solid foods, especially when pieces of sediment or small solids need filtration. This piece of equipment might come in handy when you need to puree or grind foods for your home canning. A blender or food processor should perform the same function too but a food strainer is my preference because it does not require electricity.

Timer: For me, a timer is mandatory for canning considering the role of timing in some aspects of the activity. For instance, you must adhere to the time specified in every recipe. As a home cook or chef, having one in the kitchen is non-negotiable. It will save you the stress of going back and forth looking at a timer out of the kitchen. This often amounts to time wasting.

Bubble remover: It is important to remove bubbles before going ahead to process the jars because it could prevent your lid from sealing perfectly. This can invite pathogens and bacteria and cause botulism or food-borne illnesses. Some people would rather use a spoon than a bubble remover. I strongly advise against this alternative, even though it technically works. For unskilled hands, and in the case of an unplanned loss of concentration, the spoon may chip or crack your jar while trying to remove the bubbles.

Citric acid: Citric Acid, a natural food additive, is good for maintaining a safe pH level in the water bath canning of vegetables and fruits. Although many fruits are high in acid, the acid may not be enough to terminate all harmful pathogens. This is where citric acid's usefulness comes in handy. It prevents spores and bacteria that can cause food poisoning from forming in the food you intend to can.

pH meter: A pH meter is a device that is used to measure acidity. This might be needed in the preparation of certain recipes. However, a home canning aficionado does not need one, particularly if they are using recipes from credible sources.

TIPS FOR PURCHASING THE SUPPLIES

Now that you have a complete list of the essential equipment for water bath canning, I have a few tips to guide you on how to procure them.

Purchase canning tool kits: Perhaps you are new to canning and your kitchen equipment does not cover much ground. I suggest you go for a canning tool kit, which comprises most of the canning tools needed for water bath canning. These include a canning jar lifter, wide funnel, measuring spoons or ladle, and canning lid. This helps you tick the boxes of the essentials.

Use what you have already: Chances are that you have some of the supplies in your kitchen. Be sure to do a small inventory of the stuff you have already. For example, if you have got a good pot, it can act as a substitute for a water bath canner. However, you need to get a fitting rack and ensure that the pot has coated handles to protect your fingers. Also, the pot should be big enough to ensure that the boiling water submerges the jars.

Do not rely on online stores for your supplies: While your supplies are easily available online, you shouldn't shy away from going to a physical store. One thing is for sure: you can see what you are buying. Returns are a lot easier and you do not need to pay extra bucks for shipping.

Get a variety of jars: The main caveat here is that you should know what you are canning. As stated earlier, you can only use the water bath canning technique for high-acid foods. This means your jars, irrespective of the size, must be of the regular-mouth type.

CHAPTER THREE

This chapter is one of the two practical divisions of this book, perhaps the dual nerve centers if you will. Remember that I had mentioned the role of good canning books in the previous chapter. Such books are designed to guide you to doing your canning right. This book is a good example. And here is part of it that could act as your canning reference point.

The focus is on the canning process from start to finish. It aims to provide clear and easy-to-follow, quick-to-understand steps to first-timers. Perhaps you have done your canning a long time ago and you need refreshers or reference points. This chapter is all you need. After all, you know the supplies needed for the activity already. Without further ado, let's get right into the steps.

WATER BATH CANNING STEP-BY-STEP GUIDE

PREPARATION

1. Assemble your supplies: This is pretty obvious and easy, right? True. However, you want to be sure you have everything that is needed. Simply list out the equipment and supplies in the previous chapter and check them out. Ask the right questions while doing this, such as where are the jars? What brands do you prefer, Kerr or Ball? How many do you need for the foods at hand? What sizes of the jar are required? Ensure you get exactly what you need.

Be sure to avoid using old-fashioned canning jars with glass lids and wire bails. The same goes for recycled mayonnaise or pickle. Even if you have got a hundred of those in your pantry, reuse them for some other activities other than canning. Nevertheless, you can always recycle your jars, as long as they are Mason.

Where is your canner or pot (with a rack), lids for each jar, jar lifter, ladle, funnel, and kitchen towel? Your bands must always be new. Also, ensure that the bands fit each jar. Depending on what you are canning, you should also assemble other optional items such as a strainer, knife, and bubble remover. You should also consider food safety in the choice of the optional gear you'd be using. There's a lot more on food safety throughout this book.

2. Clean up your supplies: The most important items to sterilize are the jars. Of course, you need to clean the pot and racks, too. This is because they could contain microorganisms just like the food you are canning. And, this could be harmful whenever you choose to eat canned food.

I prefer to start my cleaning with the countertop. It is the surface where the preparation of the food before placing it in jars takes place. You want to be as tidy as possible. Use soapy water to wipe the surface before proceeding to sterilize the jars, pot, rack, funnel, and tongs. Wash them in soapy water.

If you are filling your jars with food and boiling them for more than ten minutes, you do not need to sterilize the jars. On the flip side, if the boiling is less than ten minutes, it is a must that you sterilize the jars. How do you go about this? Simply place them in boiling water in a canner or pot for a minimum of ten minutes. Do this right before the jars are filled.

You do not need to boil the other tools. Place all of them in a clean large container and pour some of the boiling water on them instead. Give it a couple of minutes to rest. Thereafter, use clean tongs to transfer them to a neat white towel. Then, dry thoroughly.

3. Prepare your food items: The next step is for you to prepare your food for canning. There are numerous recipes you can choose from. I have compiled some of these recipes in the next chapter. Just before you start preparing the food, fill the pot or canner with clean water about 1–2 inches above the top of the jars.

HEATING

4. Preheat the water: This step is a bridge between food preparation and the water canning boiling process. If you're canning "hot-packed foods", preheat the water to 180 degrees Fahrenheit. If your food is "raw-packed food", preheat the food to 140 degrees Fahrenheit.

5. Load the canner: Fill the jars with a prepared recipe using a ladle and funnel to reduce or eliminate messing up your countertop. Then, load the jars into the rack and place them into the canner. Ensure that the lids are properly fitted to the jars.

6. Begin boiling after filling the jars: The recipes vary and, as such, require different boiling times. However, the common thing is to boil the filled jars for ten minutes, more or less. Start the process by turning up the heat up to warm the water. Of course, that is after covering the canner or pot. Once you have noticed that the water has begun to boil, start your timer. Remember, timing, per instructions in the recipes, is of the essence.

7. Monitor the boiling process: This step is important as well. While maintaining a boil during the scheduled time, you might need to add water to the canner just to ensure the jars are submerged.

COOLING

8. Turn the heat off: After the water has boiled through the scheduled time, turn off the heat. Remove the lid of the canner. Do not remove the jars until after five minutes.

9. Remove the jars for cooling: Remove the jars using a jar lifter and place each of them on a clean towel to prevent damage to your countertop. Ensure there is an inch space between each jar. Avoid retightening the lids to avoid seal failures.

10. Wait for 12 to 24 hours: Allow the jars to cool off for 12–24 hours. I advise waiting for the full 24 hours. Also, ensure that the cooling is done at room temperature.

STORING

11. Test the jar seals: Testing the seals is the first storage step. It is quite critical because if a jar is not properly sealed, air would enter the jar slowly over time and potentially make the content unsafe for consumption after storage. There are a few options for testing the jar seals. I recommend the following: remove the screw band and use the base of a teaspoon to tap the lid. A dull sound from the tapping is an indication that the lid is unsealed. You can also remove the screw band and press a thumb on the middle of the lid. The lid should be adjudged as unsealed if the lid springs up after pressing a thumb on it.

12. Rinse the jars: Once the sealed jars have been confirmed, dry with a clean towel. You should proceed to refrigerate any unsealed jars and consume the contents after a few days. If you wish to eat the food much later, perhaps in a week or two weeks, put it in a freezer.

13. Label with the date and item: Why is labeling necessary? Well, you need a couple of details to determine the length of storage. Some items are not meant to be stored beyond twelve months. If left unlabeled, you would be unsure of the safety for consumption after a long time. This is also the same reason why packed food items have expiry dates on their labels.

14. Proceed to store the jars: Depending on what you like, arrange the jars in a dry place, preferably in your pantry or a cool kitchen cupboard. The jars are shelf-stable for a minimum of twelve months.

There are some caveats, though. Do not store the jars near a furnace, close to hot pipes, under a sink, in direct sunlight, in an attic that is not insulated, or in any damp space. Storing the jars under any of these conditions could spoil the canned food. Avoid storing the jars at a temperature that is above 95 degrees Fahrenheit.

CHOOSING THE COOKING SURFACE

There are different cooking surfaces, all of which are quite functional. But then, some people often get confused about which one is best for their cooking style and certain cooking processes. For instance, many people have wondered which cooking surface is ideal for canning. Do you use an electric cooktop, induction cooktop, or gas range top? Irrespective of your preferences, I want to be clear that some cooking surfaces are a no-no for canning, especially pressure canning.

A camping cooker is a good example. The main concern with this kind of surface is the weight your canner would bear on it. As you know, the jars with filled foods submerged in boiling water give the canner a lot of weight. This can be too much for the burner to handle. Also, a camping cooker can burn out the water in your canner too quickly, which is not something you want during canning. It can also damage the canner, particularly a pressure canner. Perhaps that is why the manuals of many outdoor camping LP gas cookers provide a disclaimer regarding canning.

Forget the life hacks you might have read from online DIY content makers. Using a dishwasher, microwave, or oven is not advised for water bath canning. They are to be taken as unsafe.

Some people resort to pouring hot fruit blends and tomatoes into jars after sterilizing them. They go on to put a lid on the jars and screw them with a screw band. Fine, you have sealed up the food content and this seems cool. However, the contents of the jars (even if sterilized) have not been well-heated to prevent toxins, bacteria, yeast, and molds from growing after storage at room temperature. You are also advised to refrain from this technique.

In addition, researchers, particularly the USDA have written off some of the new multi-cookers even if they are designed with a canning feature. They are designated as not safe for home canning.

I believe you can perform your water bath canning on either a glass stovetop or an electric stovetop. The two types of glass stoves are good for canning. However, there are certain concerns about this cooking surface when it comes to water bath canning.

First, if your canner has an indented bottom, the heat from the glass top would be prevented from distributing sufficiently while processing. And, of course, the glass may overheat as a result of the heat reflecting from the canner to the glass. This may crack the glass, trigger the burner to shut off and leave your canner contents under-processed.

Secondly, there is the issue of being overweight which could impact the entire process. And then, dragging the canner might scratch the stove surface, potentially damaging it to an extent.

The same thing can be said about electric stovetops. Its suitability for canning depends largely on the brand you have got. Nevertheless, I recommend a coiled electric stove as opposed to the flat surface ones. Simply ensure that the pot or canner you are using is two inches beyond the coiled element across the board. Avoid using a canner with a rippled surface to ensure it contacts the heating element.

So, if you are going to use a glass cooking surface, you need to check with the manufacturer for its suitability. I am certain that one or two brands of glass cooking stoves are out there online. Just do your research thoroughly. A lot of care needs to be exercised while using a glass stovetop for water bath canning.

WATER BATH CANNING RULES

At this point, you must be wondering why water bath canning comes with many guidelines and rules. It's all about food safety. The government suffers no fools gladly when it comes to food safety. If manufacturers' food packaging is stringently regulated, it reflects the government's concern about the well-being of the citizenry. This is the reason why the USDA has made its guide to home canning a public document. I believe it makes sense to conclude this chapter by spelling out the rules, some of which have been stated earlier.

Get and use the right canner: The first thing to consider is the canner you'd be using. You can only use a water bath canner for high-acid foods. If you do not own or cannot afford to purchase one, you can use a large pot as an alternative.

Select the right jars: You should consider selecting the right jars, too. The recommended size for water bath canning is different from pressure canning. I have highlighted them in Chapter Two (check for reference). While it is okay to use the quart size canning jars or the pint size, be sure to avoid using those that are larger than a quart size.

Do not reuse lids: It is also important to get good lids with the compound under them. More importantly, endeavor to use the lids just once. This is because used lids are unreliable for a second sealing. So, do not go the penny-wise route.

Keep everything super clean: Prepare your working area, mainly a countertop, but make sure that the place is sparkling clean. Also, ensure to sterilize all the tools you need.

Take note of headspace: Getting it right with the headspace is very important. Headspace refers to the space between the jar rim and the top of the food. The rule is that you allow the right amount of headspace between the jar lid and the food (along with the liquid over it). This is in a bid to ensure proper sealing. Usually, the recipes give specific instructions regarding the headspace.

Do not make the lids too tight: One should indeed be safe while canning. However, tightening the lids too much might not build the required vacuum seal.

Be sure of the right foods: As noted in the previous chapters, not all foods can be canned through the water bath canning technique. Only high acidic foods are recommended for water bath canning.

Find reputable sources for guidance and recipes: If you checked the internet, you'd never run short of sites with water bath canning recipes. You cannot afford to rely on all of them. This book contains the best recipes sourced from reliable resources. You need not look further than it for your recipes.

Follow the recipes religiously: It is not enough to find good recipes. You need to read each of them and know what should be done before canning. Sometimes, it might be requested of you to get some special tools to execute certain steps. For instance, if you wish to can tomato sauce, you will need to get a food mill.

Label each jar: Just like I said before, labels are important to home-canned food. It provides vital information that might come in handy in the future. A paper tape is sufficient for this step.

Can at the right time: Try not to start counting the processing time until the water in the canner has come to a rolling boil. Let me reiterate this: timing is of the essence when it comes to canning. This underpins the need to have a timer close by. Use it and stick to the recommended time.

CHAPTER FOUR

One of the things I find exciting about home canning is the fact that it is a place where food preparation meets with food preservation. Imagine preparing food today and preserving them for consumption a couple of months later! That's pretty amazing, isn't it? Preparation is done before canning.

I have provided a comprehensive background to water bath canning and steps for anyone new to the whole thing. Now is the time to put you through some recipes of food to can using this method.

WATER-BATH CANNING RECIPES

Jams Marmalades, Chutneys, and Jellies

1. Strawberry-Banana Jam

Preparation time: 35 minutes

Cooking time: 10 minutes

Ingredients

- 300g banana, peeled and mashed, 1¼ cups mashed, 10 oz measured after mashing

- 700g strawberries, mashed 24 oz, 2¾ cups after mashing

- 4 tablespoons lemon juice, bottled

- 3 teaspoons Pomona Pectin

- 1 tablespoon calcium water

- 125ml honey, ½ cup/4 oz/1 teaspoon liquid stevia

Instructions

Step 1: Mash bananas and add to a large pot.

Step 2: Mash strawberries and add to the pot.

Step 3: Add calcium water to the mix and stir.

Step 4: Add your lemon juice into a sizeable bowl.

Step 5: Add the pectin powder to the content, whisked in.

Step 6: Add either the honey or liquid stevia and set aside.

Step 7: Bring the pot to a boil and add the pectin mixture, using a teaspoon at a time and stirring till all is dissolved.

Step 8: Once all ingredients are in, let it boil for two minutes maximum, and remove it from the heat.

Step 9: Ladle into ½ US pint/8 oz jars.

Step 10: Leave 1cm (¼ inch) headspace, "De-bubble", and adjust headspace.

Step 11: Wipe jar rims and put the lids on.

Step 12: Process in a water bath. You can use a steam canner instead.

Step 13: Process for 10 minutes, increasing the time as needed for your altitude.

2. Blackberry Jelly (without pectin)

Preparation time: 1 hour

Cooking time: 10 minutes

Ingredients

- 3 cups sugar
- 4 cups juice, made from 9 cups or 2½ quarts of berries and 1 cup of water

Instructions

Step 1: Add ¾ cup of sugar for every cup of blackberry juice.

Step 2: Pour the juice mixture into a deep jam pot and bring to a boil over high heat.

Step 3: In about 6–8 minutes maximum, the mixture should reach a gel state. Test for gel state/stage with an instant-read thermometer (220 degrees Fahrenheit at sea level). You can do the testing on a plate removed from the freezer.

Step 4: Once you have ascertained the gel state, transfer the mixture into prepared jam jars, be sure to allow ¼ inch headspace in each jar.

Step 5: Seal each jar with 2-piece lids.

Step 6: Use the water bath canning procedures to store long-term. Alternatively, you might store it in the refrigerator for immediate use, or freezer for up to six months.

3. Sour Cherry Jam

Preparation Time: 10 minutes

Cooking time: 45 minutes

Ingredients

- Juice of 1 lemon (2 tablespoons)
- 2 cups sugar
- 3 lbs sour cherries (5 cups pitted or 2½ lbs pitted)

Instructions

Step 1: Pit the fresh 3lbs sour cherries. If you have your fruit pitted already, ensure that the total weight is roughly 5 cups of pitted fruit or 2½ lbs pitted.

Step 2: Put your fruit in a jam pot along with the lemon juice and bring to a boil over medium-high heat.

Step 3: Cook the mixture, stirring continuously for roughly 20 minutes until the fruit has completely fallen apart.

Step 4: Add your sugar. Assuming you like to use pectin, add it at this point.

Step 5: Let the jam cook until it reaches the gel stage or an additional 25–30 minutes.

Step 6: Test for gel state/stage with an instant-read thermometer (220 degrees Fahrenheit at sea level). You can do the testing on a plate removed from the freezer.

Step 7: Ladle jam into prepared jars after turning off the heat.

Step 8: De-bubble the content of the jars, wipe the rims, and adjust headspace to ¼ inch.

Step 9: Process in a water bath canner for 10 minutes for a shelf-stable jam. Alternatively, you can store it in the refrigerator for immediate use or for one-month of storage maximum.

4. Green Mango Chutney with Whole Spice

Preparation time: 20 minutes

Cooking time: 35 minutes

Ingredients

- 2 tablespoons fennel seeds
- 6 pounds green mangoes
- 1 tablespoon whole black peppercorns
- 1 tablespoon green cardamom pods, crushed slightly

- 2 teaspoons whole cloves

- 4 teaspoons fenugreek seeds, crushed

- 2 teaspoons cumin seeds

- 4½ cups sugar

- 1 teaspoon ground cinnamon

- 2 small hot green chilies minced (alternatively use jalapenos, serrano, or habaneros)

- 4 teaspoons kosher salt

- 1 cup distilled white vinegar (5 % acidity)

Instructions

Step 1: Prepare your canning supplies. Ensure your jars are sterile and kept warm. Place your lids in a warm saucepan, too.

Step 2: After washing and peeling your mangoes, slicing each in half lengthwise and cutting them into quarter-inch long pieces. Set aside in a bowl.

Step 3: Add fenugreek, cardamom, cloves, cumin, peppercorns, and fennel to a stainless steel 6–8 quart pot.

Step 4: Add ½ cup water, sugar, cinnamon, salt, mangoes, and chilis. Stir ingredients until well-combined.

Step 5: Bring the mixture to a boil, while stirring repeatedly.

Step 6: Lower the heat to a brisk simmer and cook the mixture for 10 minutes.

Step 7: Skim the foams off the top of the cooking mixture, stirring occasionally.

Step 8: After the mango has turned translucent, add vinegar and return to a quick simmer.

Step 9: Cook the content for another 20–25 minutes. Be sure to stir intermittently.

Step 10: After the mangoes have fallen apart totally and the liquid has thickened, turn off the heat.

Step 11: Ladle hot chutney into the jars, leaving ¼ inch of headspace.

Step 12: De-bubble and wipe the rim of the jars before proceeding to place a lid on each jar.

Step 13: Proceed to water bath canning the jars. If you are using half-pint jars, process for five minutes. If you are using quart jars, process for ten minutes. Ensure that you adjust processing time for altitude.

Step 14: Remove the jars after processing and leave them to rest on a towel for a minimum of twelve hours. Proceed to storage measures.

5. Gooseberry Jam

Preparation time: 20 minutes

Cooking time: 20 minutes

Ingredients

- ¾–1lb sugar (1½ to 2 cups)
- 1lb gooseberries (roughly 3 cups)
- ¼ cup water
- 1–2 tbsp lemon juice (not compulsory)

Instructions

Step 1: Clean each of the gooseberries by removing their tails and tops.

Step 2: Put the cleaned gooseberries into a pot already filled with the water and lemon juice. Bring them to a boil over medium-high heat for about five minutes.

Step 3: Add the sugar to the mix and boil until it reaches the gel stage, about ten minutes.

Step 4: Test for gel state/stage with an instant-read thermometer (220 degrees Fahrenheit at sea level). You can do the testing on a plate removed from the freezer.

Step 5: Pour the jam into prepared jars, leaving ¼ inch headspace, apply 2-piece lids, and seal finger tight.

Step 6: Process the jars of gooseberry jam in a water bath canner for ten minutes. You may store them in the refrigerator for immediate use.

DESSERTS

6. Mock Canned Pineapple (chunk or crushed)

Preparation time: 65 minutes

Ingredients

- 46 ounces canned unsweetened pineapple juice
- 10 cups zucchini (shredded or cubed, peeled, seeds removed)
- 1½ cups bottled lemon juice, necessary for safe canning
- Yellow food coloring, for eye appeal
- 3 cups sugar
- 1 pinch salt
- ½ cup coconut rum (not compulsory) or ½ cup pineapple rum (not compulsory)
- 1–2 teaspoon coconut, extract to taste (not compulsory)

Instructions

Step 1: Shred the zucchini for crushed pineapple, or cube for chunks. The chunks will fill more jars than the shredded ones.

Step 2: Place the shredded zucchini in a strainer for fifteen minutes and squeeze out excess water afterward.

Alternatively, place the cubed zucchini in a strainer, lightly salt, toss, and let it sit for twenty minutes.

Step 3: Rinse, drain, and dry with paper towels.

Step 4: While the zucchini is draining, place juices, sugar, salt, and food coloring in a large pot and bring it to a boil.

Step 5: Add shredded zucchini to the pot and bring it back to a boil for twenty-five minutes. You need to boil for forty minutes if your zucchini is cubed.

Step 6: After that, if you are using extract and rum, add and cook for additional five minutes.

Step 7: Ladle the hot mixture and cooking liquid into sterilized jars, leaving ½ inch of headspace.

Step 8: Remove air bubbles, wipe jar rims, and adjust lids.

Step 9: Process in a boiling water bath. If the jars are half-pints or pints, you need to process them for fifteen minutes.

7. Blueberry-Lemon Dessert Sauce

Preparation time: 15 minutes

Cooking time: 15 minutes

Ingredients

- 4 cups (2 pints) fresh blueberries
- 1 teaspoon fresh lemon zest (roughly 1 lemon)
- 3 cups (22.5 ounces) granulated sugar
- 1 tablespoon fresh lemon juice (roughly ½ lemon)
- 3 ounces (1 pouch) Ball Liquid Fruit Pectin

Instructions

Step 1: Prepare your jars, lids, and bands by washing and sterilizing them.

Step 2: Rinse the blueberries, sort to remove stems or debris, and set in a strainer to drain.

Step 3: Fill a 10-quart stock pot with water (¾ full), place on burner over medium-high heat, and bring the water to a simmer.

Step 4: In the meantime, transfer the berries to a heavy-bottomed stainless-steel pot or 6-quart enameled Dutch oven. Then, use a spoon or potato masher, or crush the berries lightly to split the skins. You need some pieces of fruit in your sauce. So, avoid mashing the berries completely.

Step 5: Add lemon zest, lemon juice, and sugar to the berries and stir to combine. Then, turn the heat to high, stirring continuously.

Step 6: Bring the contents to a rolling boil which cannot be stirred down.

Step 7: Without delay, squeeze the entire contents of liquid pectin from the pouch into the boiling pot and continue boiling for an additional minute, stirring constantly.

Step 8: Remove from heat and skim off any foam, if need be.

Step 9: Ladle the hot mixture into hot jars, ensuring ¼ inch headspace.

Step 10: De-bubble, wipe the rims of the jars, and put a lid on each of them.

PICKLES

8. Bread and Butter Pickle

Preparation time: 1hr 45 minutes

Cooking time: 15 minutes

Ingredients

- 2 pounds yellow onions, thinly sliced.
- 4 pounds cucumbers, preferably Kirby pickling cucumbers
- 1/3 cup salt, preferably preservative-free
- 3 cups sugar
- 2 teaspoons ground turmeric
- 2 tablespoons yellow mustard seeds
- 1 teaspoon ground ginger
- 2 teaspoons celery seeds
- 3 cups white vinegar, 5% acidity
- 1 teaspoon whole black peppercorns
- 1 teaspoon "Pickle Crisp" (not compulsory)

Instructions

Step 1: Rinse the cucumbers under cold water, using a colander, drain, and transfer to a big bowl.

Step 2: Carefully remove the stem and blossom the end of each of the cucumbers.

Step 3: Cut the cucumbers crosswise into ¼-inch slices, placing the slices into a strainer that you have placed over a bowl to trap any liquid drippings.

Step 4: Then, add sliced yellow onions to the strainer that contains the sliced cucumbers and toss the whole mixture with salt.

Step 5: Let the mixture drain at room temperature for an hour and a half.

Step 6: Once the draining process is complete, combine spices, sugar, and vinegar in a large enameled or stainless-steel stockpot or saucepan.

Step 7: Bring the mixture to a boil, stirring till the sugar dissolves. Afterward, add the un-rinsed onions and cucumbers, along with any liquid that has drained into the bowl, into the stockpot/saucepan.

Step 8: Bring the mixture back up to a boil and stir vigorously. Remove from heat as soon as the mixture reaches a boil.

Step 9: Ladle the hot brine and pickles into your jars leaving ¼ inch headspace. Ensure the jars are still hot when you fill them with the brine and pickles. Proceed to water bath can to store for a year. Alternatively, you can refrigerate it for use for up to six months.

9. Sweet Pickle Relish

Preparation time: 25 minutes

Cooking time: 25 minutes

Ingredients

- 2 cups onions, chopped
- 1 quart chopped cucumbers
- 1 cup red bell pepper, chopped
- 1 cup green bell pepper, chopped
- ¼ cup salt
- 1 tablespoon celery seed
- 3½ cups sugar
- 2 cups apple cider vinegar
- 1 tablespoon mustard seed

Instructions

Step 1: Preheat the oven to 225 degrees, after you have cleaned your jar. Further sterilize the jars by placing them on a baking sheet and baking in your oven for a minimum of twenty minutes.

Step 2: Add the jar lids and rings to a small saucepan filled with water. Bring water to 180 degrees Fahrenheit, cover, and take away from heat.

Step 3: Combine bell peppers, cucumbers, and onions in a large bowl.

Step 4: Sprinkle the combination with salt, cover with cold water, and let it rest for two hours.

Step 5: Drain the liquid and rinse well, separating as much water as possible from the vegetables.

Step 6: Proceed to combine the spices, sugar, and vinegar in a saucepan and immediately bring to a boil.

Step 7: Then, add the drained vegetables and let simmer for exactly ten minutes.

Step 8: Put the hot relish into your jars, allowing ¼ inch headspace at the top of the jar.

Step 9: Remove any air bubbles, and secure your lids on the top of the jars.

Step 10: Proceed to process in a water bath canner for ten minutes. Lift jars out afterward, dry off and allow them to cool.

TOMATOES

10. Rotel-style Tomatoes

Preparation time: 40 minutes

Cooking time: 1hr

Ingredients

- 8 tablespoons bottled lemon juice
- 5 pounds Roma or paste tomatoes
- 2 Poblano peppers

Instructions

Step 1: Get and clean four 12-ounce jelly jars. Place the lids in a small saucepan, pour water to cover them, and let them simmer over low heat.

Step 2: Line a rimmed baking sheet with aluminum foil and preheat your broiler. Arrange the poblano peppers on the baking sheet and roast them under the broiler for four minutes. After one side darkens, turn the peppers, until all sides are blistered and blackened.

Step 3: Take out the peppers from your oven and cover them with a separate sheet of foil. Allow them to cool to the point that you can handle them. Then, remove the skins and seeds, dice the peppers afterward.

Step 4: Bring a large pot of water to a boil. Meanwhile, remove the cores from your tomatoes and score the bottoms with a shallow "X". Then, fill a large bowl with 2/3 cold water and place close to the stove.

Step 5: Blanch all your tomatoes in batches for 1–2 minutes. Allow the water to come back to a boil between each batch. Immediately after each batch is done, transfer them to the bowl of ice using a slotted spoon.

Step 6: Once all the tomatoes have been blanched and they are cool enough to touch, remove the skins.

Step 7: Chop the peeled tomatoes and put them in a pot. Then, add the diced poblanos and bring them to a boil.

Step 8: Move to cook at a monitored boil for 30–45 minutes, stirring frequently to avoid burning.

Step 9: Add two tablespoons of bottled lemon juice to the bottom of each jar and pour the hot chopped tomatoes in, leaving ½ inch of headspace.

Step 10: Get your bubble remover to remove air bubbles that surface. A wooden chopstick can work, too. Then, adjust the number of tomatoes, as necessary.

Step 11: Wipe the rims of jars, put a lid and ring on each of them, and process in a boiling water bath for thirty-five minutes.

Step 10: Remove the jars to cool and test the seals afterward. Remember to refrigerate jars with unsealed lids and use as soon as possible.

11. Grandma's canned Tomatoes

Preparation time: 5 hours

Cooking time: 1 hour

Ingredients

- 4 teaspoons Kosher salt
- 12 pounds ripe tomatoes
- 4 sterilized quart jars with lids and rims
- 4 tablespoons bottled lemon juice

Instructions

Step 1: For easy peeling, cut an "X" into the bottom of each tomato. Boil a large stockpot pot of water and add all the tomatoes to it, doing this in batches if needed.

Step 2: Once the skins of the tomatoes begin to retract after a minute, remove them from the water and plunge them into cold water.

Step 3: Cut out the stems of the tomatoes after peeling the skins off. Then, press the peeled tomatoes firmly into your sterilized jars, so that only ½ inch remains at the top.

Step 4: As soon as the jars are filled, add a tablespoon of bottled lemon juice and a teaspoon of Kosher salt to each quart. Then, place and tighten the lids and rims on the jars.

Step 5: Proceed to prepare a large boiling water bath in a stockpot pot, ensuring that the water is deep enough to cover the jars.

Step 6: As soon as the water comes to a boil, use a wire rack to lower the jars into water. Let the jars process in the water bath for exactly forty-five minutes. Monitor the water to know if there is a need to add more.

Step 7: Once the processing is done, remove the rack cautiously and place it on a heatproof surface. Then, cover the jars with a clean dishtowel, and let them cool at room temperature for a few hours.

Step 8: Test the seals, label the jars with the name of the contents and date, and store in a cool, dark place.

12. Sweet and Savory Tomato Jam

Preparation time: 10 minutes

Cooking time: 3hrs 20 minutes

Ingredients

- 1 small onion, chopped
- 3½ pounds tomatoes, coarsely chopped
- ½ cup brown sugar
- 1 teaspoon salt
- 1½ cups granulated sugar
- ½ teaspoon coriander
- ¼ cup cider vinegar
- ¼ teaspoon cumin
- 1 lemon, juice of

Instructions

Step 1: Assemble all the ingredients in a two-quart pot, bring to a gentle boil, and reduce the heat to a simmer.

Step 2: Then, cook the mixture until it becomes thickened to a jam-like consistency, roughly three hours.

Step 3: Transfer the mix to sterilized glass jars and process through water bath canning for exactly fifteen minutes. Alternatively, you may store it in the refrigerator for up to two weeks.

CONDIMENTS

13. Maple walnut syrup

Preparation time: 15 minutes

Cooking time: 30 minutes

Ingredients

- 250 ml maple syrup (1 cup / 8 oz)
- 375 ml corn syrup (1½ cups / 12 oz)
- 100g white sugar (½ cup / 4 oz)
- 125 ml water (½ cup / 4 oz)
- 200g walnut pieces (2 cups / 8 oz)

Instructions

Step 1: Put the maple syrup, corn syrup, and water in a large saucepan off the heat. Stir well.

Step 2: After stirring well, add the sugar and continue stirring until the sugar dissolves.

Step 3: Bring the mix to a boil on the stove, stirring regularly.

Step 4: Reduce to a simmer and continue to simmer uncovered for approximately fifteen minutes until it thickens a little. Stir frequently.

Step 5: Stir in the walnuts and simmer for an additional five minutes.

Step 6: Ladle the content into ½ pint jars and allow ¼ inch headspace.

Step 7: De-bubble, wipe the jar rims and put the lids on.

Step 8: Proceed to process the jars in a water bath canner for ten minutes, increasing the time required for your altitude.

14. Banana Ketchup

Preparation time: 10 minutes

Cooking time: 45 minutes

Ingredients

- 1 large onion, chopped (about 2 cups)
- 2 cups mashed bananas
- 2 teaspoons grated ginger, fresh
- 3 garlic cloves, minced
- 1 cup water, divided
- 1–2 bird's eye chilis, chopped
- 2 tablespoons tomato paste
- ¾ cup sugar
- 1 cup apple cider vinegar
- ½ teaspoon turmeric
- ½ teaspoon allspice
- 2 tablespoons bottled lemon juice
- ¼ teaspoon cinnamon

Instructions

Step 1: Sauté garlic and onion in ¼ cup of water over medium heat until soft. Cook at a simmer after adding the remaining ingredients, stirring continuously until thickened. Do this for roughly fifteen minutes.

Step 2: While the sauce is cooking, prepare your boiling water bath. Heat jars in simmering water until ready to use. Avoid boiling. Set the lids aside after washing them in warm soapy water.

Step 3: Using an immersion blender or in the bowl of a food processor, puree until smooth.

Step 4: Start ladling the hot ketchup into a hot jar, leaving ½ inch of headspace.

Step 5: De-bubble, wipe the jar rims and put the lids and bands on.

Step 6: Process the jars for twenty minutes, ensuring that you adjust for altitude.

15. Apple Cider Syrup

Preparation time: 10 minutes

Cooking time: 20 minutes

Ingredients

1 Gallon Apple Cider, preservative-free

Instructions

Step 1: Pour the apple cider into a Dutch oven or six-quart non-reactive stockpot. Avoid using copper or aluminum.

Mark the depth of the cider on a wooden skewer.

Step 2: Bring the cider to a boil and cook for roughly thirty minutes.

Step 3: Pour the cider through a mesh strainer to separate the pectin.

Step 4: Then, clean the pot and return the filtered cider to it.

Step 5: Return the cider to a boil and turn the heat down to medium-low.

Step 6: Simmer the cider for 4–6 hours, until it has reached one-seventh of its original volume just as measured on a wooden skewer. You may use an instant-read thermometer as an alternative.

Meals in a Jar

Breakfast

16. Whole Cranberries

Ingredients

- Cranberries and water
- Sugar (optional)

Instructions

Step 1: Prepare your canning jars, lids, and a water bath canner.

Step 2: Wash and prepare the cranberries, taking time to pick them over to remove any damaged fruit.

Step 3: Bring water, canning syrup, or juice to a simmer in a separate pan.

Step 4: Add the cranberries to the simmering liquid and gently simmer for 1–2 minutes.

Step 5: Ladle the cranberries into your prepared jars, topping with the canning liquid from the pot to allow ½ inch headspace.

Step 6: Proceed to seal with 2-part canning lids and process in a water bath canner for fifteen minutes. Ensure your canning time is adjusted for altitudes above 1000 ft.

Step 7: After that, turn off the heat and allow the jars to remain in the hot water for another five minutes to cool a bit.

Step 8: Remove the jars from the canner and let them cool on a towel, undisturbed for roughly twenty-four hours.

Step 9: After that, test the seals and store. Put any unsealed jars in the refrigerator for immediate use.

17. Apple Jam

Preparation time: 4 hours

Cooking time: 20 minutes

Ingredients

- ½ cup lemon juice (fresh or bottled)
- 16 cups apple pieces, peeled, cored & diced (4 lbs prepared, from about 6 lbs whole apples)
- 4 cups sugar (2 lbs)

Instructions

Step 1: Take the apple pieces, peel, core, and dice them into chunks (about ¼ to ½ inch cubes).

Step 2: Toss the chunks of diced apples in lemon juice and sugar. Cover and refrigerate it overnight for 12–24 hours. With this step, the fruit will retain a chunky texture.

Step 3: Prepare a water bath canner.

Step 4: Bring the mixture to a boil over high heat in a heavy-bottomed saucepan. The pan should be big enough to handle the foaming of the mixture and ensure it does not overflow.

Step 5: Stir the mixture intermittently, managing overflow. Cook for 20–30 minutes.

Step 6: Continue cooking until the apple jam reaches the gel stage. Use an instant-read thermometer to test a small amount of the jam for the gel stage. Alternatively, do the testing by placing a small amount on a plate and place in the freezer. The gel stage is expected at 220 degrees Fahrenheit.

Step 7: As soon as the jam reaches the gel stage, remove it from the heat and pack it into jars leaving ¼ inch headspace.

Step 8: Seal the jars with 2-part canning lids.

Step 9: Proceed to process in a water bath canner for ten minutes.

Step 10: Turn off the heat and allow the jars to sit for another five minutes before transferring them to a towel on the counter.

Step 11: Check for seals after a few hours. Store any unsealed jars in the refrigerator for immediate use and the properly sealed jars in a cool and dry place for long-term storage.

18. Ground Cherry

Preparation time: 5 minutes

Cooking time: 15 minutes

Ingredients

- 3 cups ground cherries, husked
- 2 tablespoons lemon juice
- 1 cup sugar

Instructions

Step 1: Remove husks from the ground cherries and add them

to a saucepan.

Step 2: Add the lemon juice and cook over low heat. After the ground cherries have popped and their juice has released, stir to break them up a bit.

Step 3: Then, add the sugar and cook over medium heat until the jam thickens, roughly fifteen minutes.

Step 4: Pour the jam while hot into clean ¼ pint Mason jars. Be sure to leave ¼ inch headspace.

Step 5: Proceed to process in a water bath canner for five minutes. Alternatively, put in the refrigerator for immediate use.

19. Blackberry Pie Filling

Preparation time: 20 minutes

Cooking time: 30 minutes

Ingredients

- 5 tablespoons Clearjel (35 g / 1¼ oz)
- 500 g fresh blackberries (1 lb / 3½ cups whole. Measured after prep with stems removed)
- 250 ml cold water (Or juice. 1 cup / 8 oz)
- 175 g white sugar (6 oz / ¾ cup plus 2 tbsp)
- 3½ teaspoons lemon juice, bottled
- 3 drops red food coloring (optional)
- 1 drop blue food coloring (optional)

Instructions

Step 1: Wash the blackberries and place them in a batch at a time in boiling water.

Step 2: Let the water return to the boil, and then boil for a minute. Remove fruit immediately and put it in a covered bowl to keep warm.

Step 3: Put the Clearjel and sugar (optional) in a large pot and mix the contents. Add water (or juice) and food coloring (optional). Stir constantly over medium heat until the mixture thickens and starts to bubble.

Step 4: Then, add lemon juice and cook for an additional minute before folding in all the berries at once.

Step 5: Ladle the hot mixture into hot (1 pint or 1 quart) jars. Leave 1¼ inch headspace.

Step 6: De-bubble, adjust headspace and wipe jar rims.

Step 7: Put lids on the jars.

Step 8: Proceed to process the jars in a water bath canner for thirty minutes.

Lunch

20. Apple Sauce

Preparation time: 20 minutes

Cooking time: 20 minutes

Ingredients

- ½ cup water (or apple juice)
- 5–7 lbs apples
- Lemon Juice (optional, 1 to 4 tbsp)
- Sugar (optional, ½ to 2 cups)
- Spices (optional, 1–2 tsp ground spices total)

Instructions

Step 1: Take the apples. Peel, core, and chop them.

Step 2: Place the chopped apples and water in a heavy-bottomed soup pot. Then cook over medium heat until the apples have cooked through, about fifteen to twenty minutes.

Step 3: Add lemon juice, sugar, and spices to taste (optional).

Step 4: If you have a chunky apple sauce, use a potato masher, or stir to break them up. If the apple sauce is smooth, process the sauce with a stick blender or food mill.

Step 5: Proceed to canning using a hot water bath canner for five minutes.

21. Cranberry Orange Jam (Marmalade)

Preparation time: 15 minutes

Cooking time: 40 minutes

Ingredients

- 4 cups fresh cranberries
- 2 large navel oranges (1.1 lbs total)
- 2 cups water
- 1 cup apple juice
- 2 small limes
- 2⅔–3 cups granulated sugar

Instructions

Step 1: Start by washing the oranges and removing the peel with a fruit peeler. Avoid peeling the white pith accidentally.

Step 2: Slice the peel into thin strips, with each one no longer than one inch. Place the strips in a Maslin pan.

Step 3: Peel the white pith off the orange and throw away. Then cut the oranges in half and remove all the seeds.

Step 4: Squeeze the juice from the orange halves into the Maslin pan. Afterward, tie the squeezed orange halves into a muslin cloth and place in the Maslin pan.

Step 5: Add water to the Maslin pan, bring to a boil and reduce the heat to a simmer.

Step 6: Simmer for thirty minutes, intermittently stirring the orange peel strips and prodding the muslin bag, until the orange peel strips become soft. Let the muslin bag continue cooking in the jam pot until the end.

Step 7: Wash the cranberries, add them to the pan along with the apple juice. Bring the pan to a boil again, and cook for about ten minutes, checking to see that all the cranberries have popped and broken apart. Use a spatula to lightly press any cranberry that remains whole against the side of the pot to pop it.

Step 8: Proceed to add in the zest and juice from the two limes and the sugar. Bring to a rolling boil, scraping the bottom of the pan from time to time to prevent the jam from sticking and burning.

Step 9: After the content has reached the setting point (220 degrees Fahrenheit), remove the pan and allow it to stand for about five minutes. Remove the muslin bag, too.

Step 10: Stir the jam gently, transfer into sterilized jars, and seal the jars immediately.

Step 11: Proceed to process the jars in a boiling water canner and store for year-long shelving. You may decide to store the jam in the refrigerator for up to two weeks instead of water bath canning.

22. Tomato and Cashew Chutney

Preparation time: 20 minutes

Cooking time: 1h

Ingredients

- 6 ounces onion, diced (roughly 1 small onion)
- 1 tablespoon vegetable oil
- 2 teaspoons brown mustard seeds
- 2 tablespoons fresh ginger, minced
- 1 teaspoon crushed fenugreek
- 1 teaspoon cumin seeds
- ½ cup diced dried mangoes, golden raisins, or diced dried apricots
- 4 teaspoons pure kosher salt
- 1 cup unroasted cashews, coarsely chopped
- 3 pounds tomatoes (Roma), peeled and diced
- 3 jalapenos, seeded and diced
- ¾ cup sugar
- ½ teaspoon ground cayenne
- ½ cup cider vinegar (5 % acidity)

Instructions

Step 1: Clean and sterilize your jars, and keep them warm. Place lids in a warm saucepan until ready.

Step 2: Add oil and heat on medium-high in a stainless-steel 6–8-quart pot. Go on to sauté the onions until soft for about three minutes and add garlic and ginger. Continue to sauté for additional thirty seconds.

Step 3: Thereafter, add cumin seeds, mustard seeds, mangoes, fenugreek, and cashews to the mix. Go on to sauté for one minute.

Step 4: Then, add the remaining ingredients, stir well, and bring to a boil. Reduce the heat to a brisk simmer and keep on cooking until fruits and vegetables become tender and thickened in texture (roughly 10–15 minutes).

Step 5: Ladle the hot chutney into your hot jars, leaving ¼ inch of headspace.

Step 6: Remove air bubbles, wipe the rim of the jars, and place a 2-part lid on each jar.

Step 7: Proceed to water bath canning the jars for thirty-five minutes. Ensure that the processing time is adjusted to your altitude.

Step 8: Using a jar lifter, transfer the jars to a clean towel placed on your kitchen countertop. Let the jars rest undisturbed for a minimum of twelve hours. Refrigerate jars that are not well-sealed.

Dinner

23. Apple Pie Filling

Preparation time: 30 minutes

Cooking time: 30 minutes

Ingredients

- 12 cups apple slices, peeled, cored, and splashed with lemon juice
- ¾ cup ClearJel, Cook Type
- 2¾ cups sugar
- ½ tsp nutmeg, ground
- ½ to 1½ tsp cinnamon, ground
- 2½ cups apple juice
- ½ cups lemon juice, plus more for treating raw apple slices
- 1¼ cups water

Instructions

Step 1: Prepare your supplies including a water bath canner, canning jars, and lids.

Step 2: Peel, core, and slice apples. Spatter lemon juice on the slices to prevent browning.

Step 3: In two batches of six cups each, blanch the apple slices in a small amount (approximately 1 quart) of boiling water for one minute.

Step 4: Strain the apple slices and keep them covered and warm while you prepare the filling.

Step 5: Combine the rest of the ingredients (except lemon juice) in a large saucepan. Bring to a boil before adding the lemon juice, return to a boil, and cook for no more than one minute.

Step 6: Add the hot blanched apple slices to the mix, stirring to incorporate them properly.

Step 7: Fill the jars with the mixture, leaving one full inch of headspace.

Step 8: Remove air bubbles, wipe the rim of the jars, and place a 2-part lid on each jar.

Step 9: Proceed to process in a water bath canner for twenty-five minutes. After turning off the canner, allow the jars to sit for 5–10 minutes.

Step 10: Remove the jars using a jar lifter and allow the jars to cool to room temperature before checking seals and storing them for a maximum of eighteen months.

Step 11: Store any unsealed jars in the refrigerator and use them within two weeks.

24. Spiced Crab Apple

Preparation time: 15 minutes

Cooking time: 20 minutes

Ingredients

- 3 cups sugar
- 1-quart crab apples
- 1½ cups water
- 1¾ cups cider vinegar
- 1 tsp whole cloves
- 1 tbsp cardamom pods

Instructions

Step 1: Wash the apples well but let the stems remain intact.

Step 2: Prick the apples gently all over using the tip of a small sharp knife or a fork.

Step 3: Combine the vinegar, water, and sugar in a pot.

Step 4: Run a rolling pin or the side of a wine bottle over the cardamom pods to gently crack them open.

Step 5: Add the cardamom (pods and seeds) and cloves to the pan and bring to a boil.

Step 6: Reduce the heat and add the apples to the pot. Then, simmer for about 5–10 minutes, depending on the size of your apples.

Step 7: Remove the apples from the hot liquid and pack them into your jars as carefully as possible.

Step 8: Thereafter, strain the pickling liquid and pour it into the jars, completely immersing the fruit.

Step 9: Proceed to process in a water bath canner or let cool, cap, and refrigerate.

25. Green or Wax Beans Dinner

Preparation time: 50 minutes

Ingredients

- 32 cups water
- 16 cups green beans or 16 cups wax beans, cut into 1-inch lengths
- ½ cup white vinegar
- ¾ cup pickling salt

Instructions

Step 1: Pack beans loosely in sterilized jars, leaving an inch of headroom.

Step 2: Bring the remaining ingredients to a boil in a large pot.

Step 3: Pour over beans, to within ½ inch of the top. Wipe edges of jars with a clean cloth and seal with sterilized lids.

Step 4: Process in a hot water bath for thirty minutes.

Step 5: Can be served heated in the liquid from the jar or drained and rinsed, then heated.

CHAPTER FIVE

So far, we have covered the step-by-step guide on the water bath technique for home canning. I tried to come across as detailed as I could be. This is because I imagine you are either a newbie at canning or someone who needs a refresher. This chapter and the succeeding ones are predicated on this assumption of mine.

Canning is a culinary activity that I love to see as a blend of science and art. The last chapter contains twenty-five recipes you can make through water bath canning. There are hundreds, maybe even thousands, of such recipes. They exemplify the artistic part of canning, the creative side.

However, canning is also science as it comes with a lot of rules, dos and don'ts, and guidelines. You need to follow many safety procedures as well. I have mentioned many of them in previous chapters.

As far as canning goes, such details are never too much. In this chapter, you will learn some of the limitations of water bath canning. You will learn more about items that cannot be canned through this method. And, of course, I will highlight mistakes to avoid when water bath canning. Let's begin with the limitations.

WATER BATH CAN LIMITATIONS

Food Type Limitations

The food you wish to store in a jar for long-term use will determine the type of method to use. This has nothing more to it than the food's safety for consumption. Canned foods are expected to last for a minimum of twelve months of shelving.

You are not advised to use the water bath method to can low-acid foods. Therefore, water bath canning limits you to high-acid foods. The next section of this chapter takes a closer look at the items that are not suitable for water bath canning.

Altitude Problem

The altitude of your residence while canning through the water bath method could affect the processing time. In other words, the recommended time may vary. I must point out, however, that the boiling temperature remains the same irrespective of your altitude. Likewise, the amount of water required to cover the jars needs no increase. It is the processing time that might be adjusted.

Temperature Issue

Some people are not sure whether the water needs to be boiling before placing the jars in it or not. This is why the kick-off temperature for the canning process has been standardized.

If the food you ladled or put in the jars is hot, the water should be at 180 degrees Fahrenheit. Conversely, the water should be at 140 degrees Fahrenheit, if the jars contain raw food. So, I recommend that you preheat accordingly. You may use a thermometer to check the temperature of the water if necessary.

Combination Recipes Limitations

One of the culinary delights that many of us fancy is the possibility of combination recipes. It refers to a single meal that contains two or more meal components. With combination recipes, we can stretch the limits of our creativity, and interestingly, our tasting experience. Since most combination foods are low-acid, water bath canning is not appropriate to preserve them.

Strict Details

No doubt, home canning is quite popular with a large percentage of people in the US and many other countries in the world. However, it is can be unsafe and deadly if not executed correctly. As a result, water bath canning is replete with many details all of which must be taken seriously.

This is one good reason why some people would rather stick to fresh foods and ditch the idea of preservation through canning. If you have attention to detail and can follow instructions to the letter, water bath canning would do wonders for you.

You should also get reliable books on home canning, especially water bath canning. Be on the lookout for new information about the safety of the procedures.

Time-consuming

Without a doubt, home canning is quite time-consuming. To water bath can properly, the processing time is often between 10–15 minutes depending on the recipe. But, preparation can take up to 3–4 hours or more than that in some cases. As such, people with busy schedules may not be positively disposed to either water bath canning or pressure canning.

Interestingly, I see food preservation at home through these methods as ideal for busy people. The only thing they need to do is sacrifice a couple of days, preferably weekends. These days are enough to load up their pantry with foods that will always come in handy after coming home late. That said, I cannot argue against the fact that it will yank off a large chunk of your time.

Broken jars and seals

The possibility of a jar breaking during the processing can be another limitation of water bath canning. More often than not, this method doesn't impact the jar as much as pressure canning. It remains a possibility, though. The rules suggest that once you stick to the recommended jars, you'd likely not experience breakage. Also, try to check each jar to certify them as crack-free before canning properly.

What about the seals? Can they break sometime after storage? The answer is yes! This phenomenon occurs after a false seal, which can occur for some reasons. It could happen when you have not properly wiped the jar rims before processing, or when the jar is not properly canned. If you put the jar into storage, the content will spoil before the expected expiration period.

Less Nutritional Value

Yes, the nutritional value of correctly canned and stored food is well-preserved. You should note that this cannot be compared to that of veggies and fruits that are fresh out of the garden. This may be a big deal to some people but not me!

I believe what is important is for you to know how to can safely and follow the steps of reliable recipes religiously. The nutritional value of your food will be well-preserved as a consequence.

Items That Cannot Be Water Bath Canned

I mentioned in Chapter three that some items are not recommended for water bath canning. By now, you know that low-acid foods are better pressure canned. You also know that fruits, tomatoes, salsa, relishes and pickles, fruit sauces, chutneys, pie fillings, and salsa are best for water bath canning.

You can use the table below as a checklist for items that are either safe or unsafe for water bath canning. I have decided to sort out the items that are a no-no for canning thereafter.

Safe for water bath canning	Not safe for water bath canning (pressure can instead)
Jams	Poultry
Berries	Dairy products (All of them)
Apples	Seafood
Plums	Meats
Citrus fruits	Peas
Jellies	Greens
Apricots	Asparagus
Foods packed with acids like chutneys and relish	Carrots
Fruit butter	Figs
Some sauces (check with recipes)	Corn
Pears	All other vegetables
Pickles	Recipes containing oil or fatty food
Tomatoes packed with acids	Tomatoes
Peaches	Beets
Figs packed with acids	Pumpkins
Some salsas (check with recipes)	Peppers

Foods That Cannot Be Canned

Some food items that can be canned by either of the two methods (under certain conditions) are not on the above table. For example, meat stocks such as chicken stock can be processed in a pressure canner. The caveat is that you strain off the fat as much as possible before proceeding to can.

Vegetables are also good for illustration. They are remarkably high in nutrients and contain almost no fat. Therefore, the temptation to process them for storage through canning is high. But then, it is never a good idea to directly can your veggies such as cauliflower, broccoli, eggplant, olives, artichokes, and several others. Doing so will make them excessively mushy and unpalatable for consumption. The caveat is that you pickle them before water bath canning.

However, some foods cannot be canned at all. They are considered highly detrimental to your health if home canned. It is best to not risk it at all no matter the temptation. Sometimes, the processing simply messes up the food items too badly for consumption. The following are the main examples.

Dairy products: Attempting to can milk or any product that contains milk is a bad idea. The main concern is the product's extremely low acidity, a characteristic that promotes the thriving of botulism spores. Apart from that, dairy products need more heat to process, making them inedible after all is said and done. Based on this fact, butter, cheese, and cream cannot be safely canned.

Lettuce: This green food is unlike most vegetables that can be canned via pickling and the water bath method. However, lettuce is an exemption. This is because there is hardly any way to preserve them for long-term storage. Anything short of eating it fresh is not advisable.

Grains: As great as grains such as rice and wheat are, they are poor when it comes to holding up well. The nutrients that make grains great are easily destroyed and the heat can not sufficiently penetrate the interiors of the grains to kill bacteria.

Purees: Whether you're thinking about cubed squash puree or cubed pumpkins, the result might be unhealthy in the long run. The problem with purees such as pumpkins is that they can cause food poisoning if canned. Your best bet is to store them in a freezer instead.

Flour and cornstarch: These items, or any food that contains them, can harbor botulism spores, too. Flour and cornstarch are known to break down acidic foods and limit the process of killing bacteria and other pathogens. Avoid pasta and noodles, too, as they will become mush at the base of the jar. I advise you to jettison the idea of canning these items once you get the temptation.

Sweets and squash: Many candies contain a high amount of fat that can hinder the process of heat distribution during canning. Marshmallows and caramel are good examples. Squash is also too soft for canning unless you want to pickle it.

Refined Beans: Some recipes claim that it is safe to can refined beans. The reality speaks to the contrary. Refined beans have a density that makes it difficult for heat to penetrate through. I believe you should just stick to dehydrating the beans.

Lard: Talking about dense fat, lard's got a lot of it, too. This makes it hard for the processing heat to penetrate the lard, creating a thriving environment for bacteria. Ordinarily, you can easily freeze your lard for a very long time. It is also interesting that lard can hold up well when stored on your counter. I believe it can stay on the shelf for roughly six months and about a year in the freezer.

Water Bath Canning Mistakes To Avoid

The Equipment

Using the water bath canner instead of a pressure canner: The most important thing to do when it comes to food preservation through canning is to plan effectively. And, this begins with knowing the food you intend to can, what best method to use, and the right equipment for the activity. Essentially, not determining whether you need a pressure canner or a water bath canner might cost you a lot. Imagine preparing your recipe for a couple of hours only to use the latter rather than the former. Such time wasting is unforgivable. You must avoid this mistake at all costs.

Using a mayonnaise jar: There is a reason why certain jars come recommended. You are preserving your food for months. If not done correctly, you could end up eating spoiled food unknowingly in the future. This is why Mason Jar, Weck Jar, Kilner Jar, and Fowler's Vacola are specifically recommended for home canning in North America, Germany, the UK, and Australia respectively. However, some people would rather use some old-fashioned jars or mayonnaise jars instead. This could be a costly mistake in the end.

Using a cracked jar: Similarly, as long as you use any brand of the recommended jar types, you can always reuse it for canning. This allowance, nevertheless, includes the caveat "reuse wisely". What do I mean? You do not want to reuse a jar that is chipped or shows any sign of a crack. If you use a cracked jar, there is a huge chance of it breaking in the boiling water or seal failure. Even when the jar makes it to your shelf, the content can spoil, particularly if temperatures drop suddenly. A chip along the rim, no matter how small, can lead to an unsealed jar. You now know the essence of meticulously inspecting your canning jars to ascertain their fitness for processing. The best bet is to avoid reusing old jars more than once.

Reusing lids: Still, on reuse, your lids must be in perfect shape. There are single-use jar lids and reusable ones. I wouldn't say that using the latter is a terrible idea. If you found yourself in a situation whereby reusing them is the only option, go ahead and use them. However, if you notice any sign of deterioration in any of the lids, make up your mind to change it. The recommendation is that you use a brand new lid for every jar, though. The adhesive on the underneath side of a lid easily wears out with reuse, potentially leading to the jar not sealing. Since everyone should be about preserving food safely, I believe using single-use lids is the way to go.

The Pre-Processing

Overfilling water above the jars in the canner: This is pretty obvious. Water measurement is an important aspect of the water bath canning method. You should, however, avoid overfilling water above the jars placed in your canner. Potentially, this can hamper the processing and produce undesirable results. What is the point of going through the hard work of preparing your foods for this kind of preservation only to flunk the process with this costly mistake? For every water bath canning process, water covering the lids of the jars must not exceed two inches. This will get the content evenly heated on every side.

Over-filling or under-filling the jar: The headspace between the top of the food and the base of the lid must be properly measured. Always fight the temptation of filling your content to the brim of your jars. More often than not, we overfill jars inadvertently. Whatever the case, it can cause seal failure. You don't want to be compelled to have your pickles, jams, and whatnot now than at the intended time in the future. The required headspace is about half an inch or, at most, an inch. Some of the recipes you will lay your hands on specify the headspace measurement to maintain. Follow the directions to the letter.

Not checking the condition of the raw food: The quality of the food you are preparing for preservation is important, too.

Once you have collected your veggies and fruits, you need to scrutinize their condition to determine whether they are fit for the process. Endeavor to use those with signs of rotting or molds for other purposes. For example, they can be handy on the compost pile. Your vegetables must be free of blemishes even in the slightest form. Likewise, your fruits should not be overripe or underripe. Taking a taste test before canning might be helpful, too. So, when it comes to water bath canning, the ingredients must be in perfect condition.

Processing

Not monitoring the water level: Not using enough water for this method is just as unacceptable as overfilling the canner with water. Make sure to fill the canner with water up to two inches above the cover of the jars to facilitate the even distribution of heat during the boiling process. However, you should endeavor to monitor the water level as often as possible. Sometimes, the boiling water may begin to dry long before the expiration of the set schedule. You do not want to make this mistake, as it could cause a negative outcome.

Using a metal spoon to remove bubbles: One of the main impediments to having a decent headspace is the occurrence of bubbles. Because this can lead to unsealed jars, it is understandable if anyone moves quickly to remove bubbles as soon as possible. Little wonder why some people would rather use a spoon to remove the bubbles by hitting the sides of the jars while ladling food into jars. The eventuality is cracking the jar and, invariably risking seal failure. Without a doubt, it is a mistake you want to avoid. Your best bet is to use a bubble remover instead.

Over-tightening the lid: I think anyone can make this mistake. Tightening the lids to a gentle resistance without over-tightening them comes with experience. Some people get this done without even thinking of the process. It's like driving a car and making the right decisions with little consciousness. If the lids are too tight before you proceed to process the jars in hot water, it will prevent air from venting out of the jars and can cause them to fail.

The Post-Processing

Not letting the jar cool: After you have removed your jars from the canner and placed them on a towel, you must avoid not letting them cool for a while before storing them. All the hard could work culminates in a very bad anticlimax! Moving the jars around might damage the food. How so? Well, the food may forcefully contact the lid and break the seal. Meanwhile, you may not be aware of the broken seal, especially when you do not subject the cover to seal tests.

Not testing the seals: That the seals may be broken without you knowing it is a fact. The main consequence of such an occurrence is spoilage over time. And you may not notice either. That explains why regulatory agencies in most countries always advise about testing seals for any kind of home packaging of consumables like food. I described two ways of testing your seal earlier in this book. You may choose to use either or both of them, depending on what you find convenient. Again, don't go water bath canning your food without checking if the sealing is perfect.

Not labeling your jar: This may seem unimportant at first. By the time you have finished canning all the jars, however, it is possible to forget what exactly is in some of the jars. I always tell newbies to label once the jar has cooled down and the seal is confirmed as good.

Storing the jars in places not recommended: First and foremost, you must ensure that the place you are storing your jars has temperatures less than 95 degrees Fahrenheit. Temperatures between 50 and 70 degrees Fahrenheit come recommended. Avoid storing your jars in direct sunlight, in an attic that is not insulated, near hot pipes, or in a furnace. On the contrary, store them in a kitchen cabinet, a closet, or under a bed. The most important thing is to check that the place does not have temperatures above 95 degrees Fahrenheit.

CHAPTER SIX

At this point, I am convinced you believe that water canning is fun, never mind the numerous dos and don'ts, rules and regulations, and guidelines attached to it. Canning through this method amounts to killing several stones birds with one stone.

Your food is preserved for a year, allowing you to enjoy fruits and veggies any time you wish. You reduce the amount of money you need to spend when some farm products are out of season. You'd have acquired an exciting hobby and activity that gives an indescribable level of satisfaction.

However, the emphasis is on engaging in this activity with a sense of purpose and understanding to not just can but can safely. Let me say this once and for all. The numerous rules for water bath canning underline the fact that safety is non-negotiable. This chapter addresses this.

WATER BATH CANNING SAFETY CONSIDERATIONS

Getting the right equipment: One cannot say this too much. Getting to work with the wrong equipment can be detrimental. Here, I would like to view equipment from two perspectives. You'd need to equip yourself with the supplies, including the ingredients and equipment. This point is where you decide whether what you plan to can is safe for canning and the recommended method for it.

Once you are certain of these, you should get the right equipment. For example, if you are canning poultry produce, you are to use the pressure canner rather than a water bath canner.

Getting recipes from reliable sources: Once you understand the steps for water bath canning, the next is to familiarize yourself with the recipes. Looking for water bath canning recipes? You'd never run short of them on the internet. There are many books in digital and hardcopy formats on this aspect of home canning as well.

But then, you must ask yourself a couple of important questions at this point. First, is this recipe from a reliable source? Secondly, can you go all the way to process your choice of recipe and get a positive outcome? These are salient questions needed to be asked to guarantee the safety of anyone consuming the food some weeks or months later.

Let's use the US for illustration. Perhaps the most reputable source for water bath canning recipes is the USDA. The agency does not just offer credible information but updates it after new research is conducted. There are a few more reliable sources such as the National Centre for Home Food Preservation, the Presto Pressure Canner Manual, and any of the American University Cooperative Extensions. Wherever you reside, be sure to study the regulations on home canning and rely on recipes from sources such as the ones listed here.

Following recipes to the letter: It is not enough to search through all the recipes and choose the ones that catch your fancy. You need to also devote attention to the details of each recipe. Once you are sure of the source of the recipes, try to stick to the provided steps. This is because many of the recipes tweak with the processing.

For example, some recipes require less than five minutes of boiling while some require way more than ten minutes. The important thing is that recipes from reliable sources contain science-based directions or instructions.

Sticking to the standard water bath processing steps: The process seems pretty straightforward. Pour or put your food in the jars; place them submerged in water in a canner; get the water to boil for ten minutes; and so on. For every step, nonetheless, there are more specific details. It is instructive that you stick to the water bath canning specifications. Perhaps you have a recipe with some tweaks to the whole thing. As I have mentioned earlier, try to follow the recipe to the letter.

Kitchen Safety

A safe kitchen does not only limit the risks of accidents. Kitchen safety is equally about cleanliness, good hygiene, and sanitation of the entire preparation area. The water bath canning method of food preservation demands kitchen safety as much as food safety. You must ensure that all the pieces of equipment required for the entire canning process are thoroughly cleaned.

For instance, wash the jars and canner before usage. You want to be sure that all contaminants have been washed off every piece of supply. As such, soap and water comes highly recommended. Cleaning up after the preservation is also important. To clean your canner, use the following steps.

Step 1: Mix 1 tbsp of vinegar with water inside the used canner. This will help clean the darkened inside surface.

Step 2: Heat the canner of water to a boil, cover it and continue boiling till all dark deposits are no longer visible.

Step 3: Wash the canner with hot soapy water. Then, rinse and dry.

You do not proceed to store the canner just anywhere. It is recommended that canners are kept in a neat, dry location in the kitchen. It is also necessary that you keep crumpled clean paper towels in the canner to eliminate odors and absorb moisture. Turn the lid upside down and place it on the canner for easy ventilation.

Food Safety

Scrutinize the raw food to ensure they have no blemishes. Sometimes, a friend whose garden has done great decides to gift you a basket full of strawberries and apples. While it is okay to appreciate the gesture, never rush to prepare all the fruits for canning. Check their condition. My rule is to do some scrutiny of any perishable food that I did not personally purchase or harvest from my garden. If you are ever going to succeed at home canning, you'd have to adjust to this reality. Believe me, it will help promote food safety.

Food Preservation Safety

These two things I wish to isolate as regards to food preservation safety. One is the issues of handling the jars, while the other has to do with the water bath itself. I wish to say a few things about each of them.

Handling the Jars: Jars are storage vessels for your food. You must be sure to use the recommended jar type such as the Mason jar in North America. After selecting your jars, you must handle them with care. This is to ensure that you do not inadvertently crack the body or chip off the rim. As you know by now, cracking a jar renders it unsafe for water bath canning purposes. Many safety precautions say as much!

Read the safety precautions for home canning over and over again. The good news is that most credible canning safety precautions are written in clear and easily understandable language. As such, no one is allowed to get sick from eating poorly canned food.

91

Handling the Water Bath: Furthermore, when it comes to home canning, it's safety first. Something as mundane as how you handle the canning is significant. This is because poor handling of the water bath process could be detrimental to food safety. Here are three tips on how to safely handle the water bath process.

Care is a necessity: You might be an expert in home canning. This does not mean that you should go about water bath canning in the auto drive. All your mind should be invested in every step. This is to avoid careless mistakes such as cracking the jars.

Your jars are like eggs: Speaking of cracked or chipped jars, you want to treat your jars like eggs. It may sound silly but every expert at home canning shares this sentiment. If at any time, they end up with spoiled food because of a cracked or chipped jar, I would consider my job unsuccessful. That is why I handle the jars with the utmost care from start to finish.

Testing the seals is a must: A seal integrity test is a must for all sealed products, whether from industrial or domestic sources. This owes to the fact that it is an integral part of food safety. If large-scale food storage requires integrity tests for seals, yours cannot be less mandatory. You should use the methods mentioned in this book to test the integrity of seals before storage.

Temperature Management

If you have not got the temperature right, your canning will not be successful. As a result, you need to take time to understand the temperature management of the process.

Bacteria, molds, and yeasts are the bad guys that thrive in acidic foods. The role of canning temperatures is to destroy these villains, thereby making it possible to can foods for a long period. As temperatures increase, the time required to eliminate the pathogens decreases.

Cooking Temperatures

Food preservation temperatures vary according to the National Center for Home Food preservation. Our concern here is the temperatures required for water bath canning. For this method, you are going to require less than 240 to 250 degrees Fahrenheit. The standard temperature for canning acidic fruits, pickles, jellied products, and tomatoes is 212 degrees Fahrenheit. However, while warming temperatures (140–165 degrees Fahrenheit) prevent the growth of microorganisms, some microorganisms could survive them. For storage, the maximum temperature for canned foods is 95 degrees Fahrenheit, though anywhere between 50 and 70 degrees Fahrenheit is considered best for all canned foods. Meanwhile, I want to reiterate that the temperatures for pre-heating your canner over the stove include 180 degrees Fahrenheit for hot-packed foods and 140 degrees Fahrenheit for raw-packed food.

Pounds To Kilograms

Sometimes, a recipe might provide certain measurement recommendations for your food during preparation for canning. If the recipe weight measurements are provided in the imperial form, a conversion to the metric measurement might be necessary for someone resident out of the United States, Burma/Myanmar, and Liberia.

Without an accurate conversion of pounds to kilogram, you might end up impacting the outcome of your canned food negatively. And, this is tantamount to risking food spoilage after storage. Not too long ago, we had to study the calculation and do it manually. This makes people prone to miscalculations. But today, all you need is to run your calculation through the search engines, especially Google, with accuracy guaranteed. So, converting from pounds to kilograms is that easy!

Pesticides

The issue of pesticides cannot be disentangled from any discussion on food safety. These chemicals help to protect crops against fungi, insects, weeds, rodents, and other nuisances that hinder agriculture. Using pesticides can protect farmers from losing their crops for the season.

Despite playing such a huge function, pesticides can harm human beings and the environment over time. It has been proven empirically that pesticides mixed with crops expose us to many health conditions. While this may not seem obvious, the effects of such chemicals on the body manifest like that of a slow poison, often taking years. For instance, cancer, birth defects, nervous system problems, ADHD, Alzheimer's disease, and other conditions have a link to pesticides.

Gardening is one of the best ways to avoid food that contains pesticides as much as possible. By growing your veggies and fruits in your backyard, you can rest assured what you are eating wasn't sprayed with chemicals. You can also commit to local farmers whom you know grow their produce organically. This is because they tend to apply minimal pesticides on their farmland.

Canning aficionados, whether newbies or experienced, can know and internalize the Environmental Working Group's "Dirty Dozen" and "Clean Fifteen" to avoid pesticide-tainted foods. The EWG is an American activist group that researches toxic chemicals, agricultural subsidies, and drinking water pollutants while advocating for corporate accountability and change in these areas.

EWG's 2021 "Dirty Dozen"

As part of its many interventions, the EWG releases its shopper's guide to pesticides produced yearly. Containing a list of fruits and vegetables ranked based on their pesticide content levels, the guide is predicated on the fact that almost 70% of non-organic American produce contains pesticide residue.

Now, the word "dirty" is not meant to discourage people from eating these foods, even if they are non-organic. The main concern is that they could impact our health negatively after many years.

Only 1 out of 10 American adults eat sufficient fruits and veggies daily, according to the Center for Disease Control and Prevention. As a consequence, people are urged to eat these hugely nutritious food items, whether they are organic or not.

Before preparing your fruits and veggies for canning, it is instructive that you clean off pesticide residues from them. To do this, simply wash each item under running water for thirty seconds.

You should consider applying this procedure to the following "Dirty Dozen" in ranked order:

1. Strawberries

2. Spinach

3. Kale, collard & mustard greens

4. Nectarines

5. Apples

6. Grapes

7. Bell & hot peppers

8. Cherries

9. Peaches

10. Pears

11. Celery

12. Tomatoes

EWG's 2021 "Clean Fifteen"

Just like the "Dirty Dozen", the EWG compiled and released a list of clean vegetables and fruits in 2021 to guide shoppers. It is safe to conclude the following items after testing proves relatively clean of pesticide residues.

1. Avocadoes

2. Sweet corn

3. Pineapples

4. Onions

5. Papaya

6. Sweet peas (frozen)

7. Asparagus

8. Honeydew melon

9. Kiwi

10. Cabbage

11. Mushrooms

12. Cantaloupe

13. Mangoes

14. Watermelon

15. Sweet Potatoes

I advise that you still go ahead to wash these items before preparing them for canning. This is because some of the "Clean Fifteen" contain pesticide residue, though considered inconsequential.

Apart from washing your veggies and fruit under running water for thirty seconds minimum, you should also cultivate the culture of buying from local farmers. Also, prices of vegetables and fruits drop in the season because they are plentiful. You should endeavor to make a bulk purchase of organic foods in season and can them for use during periods of scarcity.

Vegetable And Fruit Water Bath Canning Charts

Charts that emanate from credible sources are good for you as an enthusiast of home canning. It is based on this fact that I decided to close this chapter with a couple of useful water bath canning charts. The first is adapted from a Utah State University Extension resource while the other is from Little Red Hen, a Non-profit Corporation Serving Children & Adults with Developmental Disabilities.

PRODUCT	STYLE OF PACK	PINT	QUARTS
FRUIT			
Apple sauce	Hot	20 Minutes	30 Minutes
Pears	Hot	30 Minutes	35 Minutes
Apricots	Hot	30 Minutes	35 Minutes
	Raw	35 Minutes	40 Minutes
Cherries	Hot	20 Minutes	30 Minutes
	Raw	35 Minutes	35 Minutes
Apple & Grape Juices	Hot	10 Minutes	10 Minutes
Peaches	Hot	30 Minutes	35 Minutes
	Raw	35 Minutes	40 Minutes
Berries	Hot	20 Minutes	20 Minutes

	Raw	20 Minutes	30 Minutes
PICKLES			
Dill Pickles	Raw	15 Minutes	20 Minutes
Dilled Beans	Raw	10 Minutes	Not Recommended
Picked Beets	Hot	40 Minutes	40 Minutes
Bread & Butter Pickles	Hot	15 Minutes	15 Minutes
Jams, Jellies & Spreads			
Jams & Jellies (With or without added pectin)	Hot	10 Minutes	10 Minutes
Spreads	Hot	20 Minutes	30 Minutes

Chart One: Culled from Utah State University Extension resource

FRUITS		
Fruit	**Measure**	**QT. Jars Needed**
Apples	48 lbs/1 bushel	16–20
Apple sauce	48 lbs/1 bushel	15–18
Apricots	22 lbs/1 lug	7–11
Berries	24 Qrts/1 crate	12–18
Cherries	22 lbs/1 lug	9–11

Peaches	48 lbs/1 bushel	18–24
Pears	50 lbs/1 bushel	20–25
Plums	56 lbs/1 bushel	24–30
Tomatoes	53 lbs/1 bushel	15–20
Tomato Juice	53 lbs/1 bushel	12–16

VEGETABLES

Vegetable	Measure	QT. Jars Needed
Beans, Green/Wax	30 lbs/1 bushel	12–20
Beans Lima (Pods)	32 lbs/1 bushel	6–10
Beets (Trim tops)	52 lbs/1 bushel	15–24
Carrots (Trim tops)	50 lbs/1 bushel	16–25
Corn (with husks)	35 lbs/1 bushel	6–10
Peas (Pods)	30 lbs/1 bushel	5–10
Pickles	48 lbs/1 bushel	16–24
Squash, Summer	40 lbs/1 bushel	10–20

CANNING SYRUPS

Syrup Type	Sugar to 1 QT. Water	Syrup Yield
Very Light	1 cup	4–1/2 cups
Light	2 cups	5 cups
Medium	3 cups	5–1/2 cups
Heavy	4-3/4 cups	6–1/2 cups

Chart Two: Culled from Little Red Hen.

CHAPTER SEVEN

I feel fulfilled that you have come along with me this far. It is safe to say you are well-informed about water bath canning, practically and theoretically. You might need some time to become an expert but starting from somewhere is a good step. There can never be too much information on home canning. It is with this sentiment that I have decided to take you through a few more things. You may choose to call it a bonus chapter. Let's dive right into it.

TYPES OF CANNERS

One of the first decisions you need to make is the kind of canner to use. This starts with the type of recipe you are making. There are two types of canners for the preservation of foods. The classification was predicated on the food that each one is being used for. Essentially, we have the water bath canner and pressure canner. If the food items in the recipe have low acidity, you're going to need a pressure canner. Conversely, a water bath canner is used for high-acid foods alone.

Water Bath Canner

This canner is a deep metal pot with a rack reaching down to the bottom and a tight cover. The rack and the depth of the pot are designed to hold jars filled with food and water slightly covering them. Using the canner requires that you leave airspace of about 1–2 inches between the cover's base and the tip of the water. This is necessary for a brisk boil.

You can use this type of canner on either a gas stovetop or an electric stove. The USDA, however, advises that anyone using an electric stove must ensure that the canner is flat-bottomed. Also, the canner must not be more than four inches wider than the heating element in diameter. Atop the burner or heating element, the canner should not go more than two inches on any side. The reason for this recommendation is to ensure even or uniform processing of the jars.

Pressure canner

There is a clear difference between a pressure canner and a pressure cooker. The latter is deployed to rapidly cook meats, making it inappropriate for any kind of home canning. It doesn't often maintain sufficient pressure and heats too quickly. On the contrary, a pressure canner is designed mainly for canning low-acid foods and appears a lot bigger than pressure cookers.

A pressure canner has the following components: an automatic vent cover lock, a removable rack, a safety fuse, and a steam vent. Ideally, your choice of pressure canner must be able to hold a minimum of four quart-size jars. Unlike the water bath canner which can be substituted with a deep pot, you are not allowed to use any other canner instead of a pressure canner. Besides, only pressure canners with the Underwriters Laboratories (UL) approval of safety symbol are considered safe.

The two types include weighted-gauge or dial-gauge pressure canners. Weighted-gauge canners have weights for five, ten, or fifteen pounds of pressure that are placed over the jiggle or vent and rock when the accurate pressure has been attained. I consider a dial-gauge canner a good choice for anyone living at higher altitudes because of the ease in making precise pressure adjustments.

Choosing Canners For Water Bath Canning

The amazing thing is that water bath canning is somewhat less difficult than pressure canning. You can rely on the equipment already in your kitchen. To attest to this, people who cannot afford a canner can simply opt for a large-sized pot which is often fit for purpose as a canner. I believe you are just as excited about canning as me. And, of course, you will be doing it for a long time. It makes sense that you get a proper water bath canner once and for all. Therefore, you consider the following factors when choosing your water bath canner.

1. Material: You need to be sure of the material you are comfortable with. Usually, most canners are made with porcelain enamel on steel, stainless steel, and aluminum. All of them have their pros and cons. For instance, stainless steel and aluminum-made canners are durable and not prone to rust. However, lower gauge aluminum canners bend easily. While porcelain steel canners are not expensive, they can chip easily, leading to rust. It's what works for you.

2. Size: This parameter for choosing a water bath canner is arguably the most important. Remember that your canner will be holding food-filled jars and water. So, you need a large canner with sufficient depth for the processing. Most people prefer to use a 21-quart pot, which can hold up to seven 1-quart jars. But there are the smaller canners and jumbo canners, too, with the latter having the capacity to hold 9-quart jars and the former 7-pint jars. The emphasis on depth hinges on the need for an allowance of 1–2 inches of boiling water above the jars.

3. Lids: Once a canner catches your fancy, be sure to check if the lid fits securely. If the lid is loose, the water will take longer to boil because of the escaping steam. Also, I would recommend that you use tempered glass which allows you to monitor the boiling process without having to lift the lid. It is even better that the lid comes with a temperature gauge or steam vent.

4. Handles: The handles must be as sturdy as the body of the canner itself. This does not mean it should be made of the same materials. Avoid getting canners made of aluminum, stainless, or porcelain steel. They might be too hot for you to use. Look out for canner with silicone-coated handles instead. You want to procure a canner with components built to withstand the hot processing.

5. Bottom Surface: This may seem unnecessary. But, just as I have emphasized many times in this book so far, every tiny detail is important in water bath canning. Here is one more seemingly mundane details to add to our growing list.

You need to take cognizance of the bottom of your canner vis-a-vis the stove in your kitchen. If your burner is electric, you should select a flat bottom canner for even heat distribution. I prefer ridged bottom surface for gas burners. This measure is to ensure good heat distribution.

Canning Storage Tips

The success of food preservation through the water bath canning process does not end with proper canning. Even if you have perfectly sealed the jars, they still need to be stored properly. This may not seem to be a big deal, especially because you have been storing stuff in the past. I want to sign a note of caution here. Storage requires as much attention to detail as the other water bath canning steps.

- Store in a cool, clean, dry place where temperatures are more than 85 degrees Fahrenheit. Avoid freezing temperatures, though.

- Avoid storing canned food for more than one year. Nevertheless, you may keep high-acid foods like pickles, tomatoes, and fruit within two years of the date labeled on the package.

- After the lids have been vacuum-sealed on the jars, remove the screw bands.

- Clean the lids and jars to remove residues of ladled food.

- Attach a label with the date and time on the jars.

- Proceed to store the jars in a neat, cool, and dry place with temperatures not above 95 degrees Fahrenheit.

- Do not store jars in direct sunlight, in an attic that is not insulated, near hot pipes, or a furnace.

- Master the spoilage warning signs of canned food. Some of the red flags are foul odor; dented, bulging, or leaking cans; and bulging or loose lids on the jars.

- If you are going to stack the jars for storage, do so with great care. You don't want the seal breaking accidentally. Try not to stack the jars, if possible.

Use stable shelves. This is because jars are heavy and can spoil shelves that are not sturdy.

CONCLUSION

At the beginning of this book, I set out to make this long read on water bath canning as detailed and expository as possible. To achieve this, I set out to provide a robust background to the topic, providing useful tips every now and then. I provided a step-by-step guide to the process and twenty-five recipes grouped into categories for easy reference. In addition, I discussed the limitations of the methods, mistakes to avoid, and safety considerations—which is, perhaps, the most significant part of canning.

This book contains nearly all the information you need to get started with water bath canning. As such many of the Frequently Asked Questions have been answered across the seven chapters. However, for emphasis, here are some of the nagging FAQs and, hopefully, answers to each of them. I would like to end by asking you to go for it. Water bath canning is safe, not as difficult as it seems, and inexpensive.

FAQs

Is it necessary to sterilize the canning jars?

It depends on the recipe you are preparing or how long you have had the jars unused. Sometimes, cleaning with soap and water may be sufficient.

Can you boil canning jars without a rack?

Unfortunately, you need a rack for all your home canning attempts. This is to keep jars from direct contact with the bottom of the canner. The heat might be too much for the glass jars and could jeopardize the entire process.

Must I use a gas stove for water bath canning?

No. You might opt for an electric stove as an alternative. The standard coil electric stove is the most highly recommended as safe for water bath canning. Simply ensure that you use a flat-bottom stockpot to ensure even distribution of heat.

What will happen if a jar breaks during canning?

There is the possibility of a jar breaking during canning. This occurrence will not hamper the processing of the other jars. Once the timer alerts you, simply use a jar lifter to take out the other jars. You only have the messed up water and clearing of the broken pieces to deal with.

Do I have to grow a lot of food for canning to be worthwhile?

Not necessarily. You can always purchase your veggies and fruits for canning from local farmers. The sizes of your purchases do not matter. Also, the amount of your harvest of homegrown food items is inconsequential.

Can I can my own salsa recipe?

Salsas are often combinations of low-acidic and acidic ingredients. You may call a salsa an acidified food. This makes it somewhat complicated for us to get the preparation right. This is depicted by the confusion one faces about which canner to use. Your best bet is to use tested recipes from credible sources like NCHFP and USDA.

Is water bath canning difficult?

You are not alone. Many experts had assumed that the method is difficult at one point or another. It is very easy as long as you have great attention to detail and can follow instructions.

Must I leave a certain measurement of headspace in the jars?

This is a good question. Without mincing words, yes! You need to leave a specified amount of headspace to guarantee a vacuum seal. Now, the emphasis is that the headspace should not be too little or too much. This explains why the most common recommendation is ¼ inch headspace.

Is water bath canning expensive?

Definitely not! All the equipment you need for the method of canning is most likely in your kitchen already. Perhaps you do not own a water bath canner. A durable large pot comes recommended as a good alternative. For me, the expensive thing about water bath canning is gaining the experience. You need to invest your time and effort in it.

THANK YOU

Just wanted to let you know how much you mean to me.

Without your help and attention, I couldn't keep making helpful publications like this one.

Once again, I appreciate you reading this book. I absolutely enjoyed writing it, and I hope you did too.

Before you leave, I need you to do me a favor.

Please consider posting a book review for this one on the platform.

Reviews will be used to help my writing.

Your feedback is extremely helpful to me and will help me to generate more. upcoming books in the information genre.

I would love to hear from you.

KAYLA.

Printed in the USA
CPSIA information can be obtained
at www.ICGtesting.com
LVHW070209210224
772423LV00013B/1117

9 781088 052846